"You make me feel alive," he said slowly

The air was charged with undercurrents of such fierce intensity that Fran's legs nearly went from under her.

"Do I make you feel that way because I shout at you and answer you back?" she asked him huskily.

"Possibly," he murmured.

"You're not used to that, are you? You command respect and subservience."

"I don't command it, but my position decrees it."

"Am I supposed to feel sorry for you?" She lifted her chin and looked at him. No, it wasn't pity he was looking for, but she read something else in his eyes. A need, a dangerous need.

NATALIE FOX was born and educated in London. She's had many interesting careers, including working in a casino as a roulette croupier, and working for a Soho coffee bar, delivering sandwiches by scooter in the West End. Although she didn't start writing until after her fortieth birthday, Natalie says she's "always been a romantic at heart." Natalie and her husband now live in Spain.

Books by Natalie Fox

HARLEQUIN PRESENTS
1473–NIGHTS OF DESIRE

NATALIE FOX

A Special Sort of Man

Harlequin Books

TORONTO • NEW YORK • LONDON
AMSTERDAM • PARIS • SYDNEY • HAMBURG
STOCKHOLM • ATHENS • TOKYO • MILAN
MADRID • WARSAW • BUDAPEST • AUCKLAND

ISBN 0-373-11653-5

A SPECIAL SORT OF MAN

Copyright © 1991 by Natalie Fox.

This edition published by arrangement with Harlequin Enterprises B. V.

® and TM are trademarks of the publisher. Trademarks indicated with
® are registered in the United States Patent and Trademark Office, the
Canadian Trade Marks Office and in other countries.

Printed in U.S.A.

CHAPTER ONE

JORDAN PARRY stood with his back to his personal assistant Silas Matthews, broad shoulders hunched with tension, taut fingers gripping the edge of the ormolu desk by the window. Paris lay beyond that window, the purple sky softening down into dusk, but Jordan took no pleasure in the view. His thoughts were on the medical conference commencing the following morning.

He glanced anxiously at his watch, frowned, and started to pace the room like a caged tiger.

Silas moved across the thickly carpeted lounge of the Monet suite and poured two hefty Scotches at the bar.

'Calm down, Jordan. Here—take this.' He handed him one of the crystal tumblers.

Jordan swivelled to face the portly older man, took the glass and gripped it unnecessarily fiercely. His grey eyes darkened with anger and concern. He swallowed his drink, and when he spoke his voice was oddly discordant. 'If those laboratory test results don't arrive tonight it will be a waste of three years' work.' He stared bleakly into the bottom of his glass. 'I can't handle this conference without those results. I can't lecture tomorrow if I've nothing to damn well sell!'

The new synthetic hormone drug they had been working on for so long was to be Jordan's last punishing bargaining power. A take-over of his arch rivals Unimet was at last in sight. Parry Pharmaceuticals was already big but Jordan wanted bigger. Now, with this new drug, they would be in an even stronger position. But Jordan wasn't fired by megalomania—his heart lay elsewhere; he was doing this out of love and respect for his late father and for his loyal employees, and the hospice his father had founded and funded all his life.

But disaster had struck, throwing the company into chaos. The computer room had defaulted badly at the eleventh hour, lost several vital pages of test results. Panic-stricken, the team had worked overnight and now the disks were on their way to Paris for the conference.

But they hadn't arrived, should have done hours ago, and fear rose like an evil serpent from the pit of Jordan's stomach.

Silas watched him anxiously, this man he had grown to love and respect as much as Robert Parry before him. The father had been born to the company, the son had been born to administering to the sick. He had been a doctor, not a businessman, but whoever in the world would have guessed it? Jordan Parry had taken over from his father and powered Parry Pharmaceuticals to even greater heights—this last new drug, if successful, would be the making of him.

Jordan raked his fingers through his thick dark hair and ran the heel of his hand punishingly down the side of his face and across his tensed jawline. Slamming his tumbler down on the desk, he picked up his horn-rimmed spectacles and reached for a sheaf of papers.

'Let's get down to these figures, Silas,' he grated determinedly. 'The disks will arrive—they have to!'

'*Excusez-moi. Je m'appelle* Cain...Francyne Cain. *Je*——'

'*Ah, oui!* Mademoiselle Cain!' The concierge of the Hotel Clermont interrupted brightly. 'You are late, yes? Monsieur Parry is most urgent for you.' He slid the register in front of her.

'*Non,*' she laughed, 'I'm Francyne. You see, my sister couldn't——' Fran was cut off in mid-sentence by a crowd of thrusting Germans, all eager to book in at the same time. They jostled against her and she gave a hopeless shrug of her shoulders and dashed off a squiggly signature in the hotel registration book. It seemed pointless trying to explain that she wasn't Jordan Parry's personal secretary Helena Cain but her sister Fran. The concierge wasn't interested in Helena's misfortune—but no doubt Parry would be, Fran thought with a small smile as she took the weighty room key offered and eased her way out of the mêlée at the desk.

She stood breathless for a while, sea-green eyes searching out the lift area. Her pulses quickened at the plushness of the elegant old hotel. So this was how her older sister lived, was it? Jet-setting around the world with her boss, the head of Parry Pharmaceuticals. Rome, Geneva and Madrid already this year and it was still only April. Fran almost envied her. It would take a week's wages from the art gallery plus her evening earnings from the wine bar to pay for just one night in this place, she reckoned, heading for the gilded lift gates.

The sombre classical music that wafted out from the lift momentarily curbed her excitement at this unexpected trip to Paris—that and the thought that she had forgotten to ask Reception for Mr Parry's room number. The lift was already chugging up to the third floor, so she made a mental note to ring down for the information as soon as she got to her room—Helena's room, she reminded herself.

Fran frowned, recalling Helena's accident that morning. It had been so unlike her sister to have thoughtlessly stepped off the kerb in Piccadilly, right into the path of a motorcycle courier. But, as Helena had weakly explained at the hospital, she was worn out after working all night and simply hadn't seen the motorbike bearing down on her when she had stepped out of the office into bright sunshine. Fortunately the young courier had seen her and braked sharply, so avoiding a more serious accident. Helena had taken a tumble in the gutter which had hurt her pride more than anything; nevertheless the hospital had decided to keep her in for observation and that was how Fran had come to be summoned to the hospital so hastily. Five floppy disks and a wadge of paperwork had to be delivered to Jordan Parry in Paris before the onset of the medical conference the following morning.

'You must do this for me, Fran,' Helena had tearfully pleaded from her hospital bed. 'Jordan needs the results of these tests we've been running on the new hormone drug. The product is ready for marketing after three years of research and the Paris seminar is its launch. He's lecturing in the morning, the first speaker—I should be with him...'

Her voice had broken dramatically at this point and it was some minutes before she could continue. Fran had waited with bated breath. 'Oh, Fran, it was my fault some of the results were lost on the computer. Everyone has been marvellous and covered for me and we worked through the night and got it right, and now this... I can't fail him a second time, Fran. You'll have to take the disks to Paris. They are of vital importance—you're the only one I can trust!'

Fran hadn't hesitated. She'd wanted to ask a hundred questions but Helena's sudden sickly pallor had vanquished them from her mind. So she had agreed, dashed home to pack a bag, phoned her two bosses to arrange a few days' leave, picked up the flight ticket Helena had hastily arranged with a phone call from her hospital bed and now here she was in Paris, creaking up to her floor at *the* Hotel Clermont and about to deliver a very precious briefcase to *the* Mr Jordan Parry, who was sure to fall over himself with gratitude.

Fran was curious to meet this phenomenon, this man who had de-iced her sister's glacial heart. He would need to be a special sort of man to satisfy Helena's needs, she mused, searching for her room number along an endless corridor. For Helena was the coldest, most calculating female she knew and, if it weren't for the fact that they were irrevocably bound by blood, Fran wouldn't be here at all.

Her room—rather, Helena's room—was beautiful. Very Parisian, very pseudo-Louis XIV. Pastel pink carpet and curtains, ornate gilded furniture. An exquisite Savonnerie rug languished expensively at the foot of the double bed with its mock Regency headboard and Fran vaguely wondered if Helena had planned on sharing that bed with her boss.

They were having an affair, of that Fran was certain. Though Helena had never admitted as much, something strange always happened to her face when she spoke of Jordan Parry. Her sister was elegantly beautiful, classically featured, never a glossy hair out of place, but that lovely yet stern countenance softened into almost girlish prettiness when the subject of her employer arose. Yes, Fran was more than curious to meet this man.

Flinging her shoulder-bag and the briefcase down on the pink silk bedcover, Fran rushed to the long window and drew back the curtains. It was dark outside, raining hard now, but because it was Paris it was somehow deliciously romantic to Fran's eyes.

The wet cobbled boulevard below gleamed like sealskin and people hurried along the wide pavements, collars high round chins. Warm golden light spilled out from half-curtained restaurants and expensively dressed shop windows, and Fran felt ripples of Paris fever quivering through her slender body.

This was her second visit to this magical city. Her first, a school trip, registered little in her mind, only misty memories of the terrifying Eiffel Tower, the pungent smell of tobacco that hung in the air and Clive Sargent getting lost on the Metro and everyone in the party secretly hoping he didn't get found—he was a pain! Now she was back, as an adult and an artist, and could see and feel anything that Paris cared to throw at her.

Impulsively Fran rummaged in her holdall for her sketch-pad and pastels. She dragged a heavy chair to the window, knotted back the fine nets and proceeded to outline the exciting street scene below. It was perfect, just the right light. Deep shadows of blue and grey, splashes of ochre and russet, an orchestration of thrilling tones ...

A telephone purred somewhere in the room but Fran was too deeply absorbed in her passion to give it attention. She'd given up her last two years of art school to nurse her sick father till his death. She'd missed out on any qualifications, missed out on a career, missed out on life in general. The gallery job, selling other people's talent, was the most she had achieved since arriving in London to live with Helena.

The telephone persisted and finally Fran gazed round the room and stared idiotically at the receiver on the bedside table. It must be a wrong number, nobody knew she was here—no one but Helena and the hospital! She flew to it, scattering pastels in every direction.

'Helena! What the hell are you doing? Reception informed me you booked in nearly an hour ago. How much longer do you need to unpack?' The voice didn't give her space to answer but thundered on. 'Come to the suite this minute!'

Fran stared incredulously at the dead receiver in her hand and then looked at her watch. *That* must have been Jordan Parry, and he wasn't wrong. She'd been here an hour and completely forgotten her reason for being in Paris. Helena would have a blue fit if she knew she had kept him waiting.

Quickly she called Reception and asked for Jordan Parry's suite number. Mercifully it was on the same floor, and grabbing the briefcase from the bed she made a dash for the door. Pastels crunched into the pale carpet under her feet.

'Oh, no!' Fran groaned helplessly. It was *his* fault! Bellowing down the phone like that, scaring her witless. She rubbed at the marks with a towel and made it worse. With a cry of frustration she dragged a heavy brocade chair over the mess and hoped the chambermaids wouldn't notice. Seconds later she was scurrying down the corridor, hot, flustered and clutching the precious briefcase to her chest.

She stopped dead outside the suite door. This was ridiculous, she told herself sensibly. Why was she panicking like a schoolgirl late for classes? This man could be her future brother-in-law.

She tapped lightly on the solid mahogany door, and while she waited for a response she mentally composed a picture of the man. Jordan Parry, Helena's lover and boss. Her sister was thirty-six, fourteen years older than herself, so Parry, if the law of averages was anything to go by, should be about six years older than Helena. About forty-twoish, but then Fran remembered Helena had said he was the chairman of this old-established company, chief shareholder too, so it was possible he was older. Yes, Fran could see him: a short, balding, ageing martinet with a voice like a clap of thunder and the telephone manners of a docker!

Fran knocked harder the next time—he was probably a bit deaf too. Still no reply. She tried the door-handle. It wasn't locked so she went in and listened for signs of life. Running water, but from where she wasn't sure. She was standing in an elegant hallway, all doors leading from it closed. Fran hesitated. Which one to take? She didn't want to barge into his bedroom, and then the choice didn't matter for she caught sight of her reflection in a gilt-framed mirror hanging on the wall. She let out a moan. Her long pale blonde hair, gathered untidily into a pony-tail and secured with frayed pink ribbon, was wispy and dishevelled. Her jeans, face and fingers were smudged with pastels, even her chunky pink sweater hadn't escaped. She was a mess!

Quickly she secured the briefcase between her knees and got to work. Leaning forward towards the mirror, she licked the tips of her fingers and started on her face. And then something caught her eye in the mirror. A pair of gleaming black leather shoes, long, impeccably tailored trouser legs. Fran straightened up, swung round and giggled at the handsome man leaning casually against the door-frame, watching her through sepia-tinted spectacles. Trust her to get caught by one of Jordan Parry's minions.

'Excuse me.' She laughed. 'Just tidying myself up for Mr Parry. I did knock but no one answered. Is he around somewhere?' She turned back to the mirror and polished off the remains of manganese blue from her chin with the back of her hand and flicked at the wisps of hair at her temples. Reaching down for the briefcase between her knees, she gave herself one last glance of approval and then, because there was no response from the man watching her, she knew. In one horrible awful second she knew.

She spun to face him, eyes wide, the smile slipping from her face. Her heel caught in the rug at her feet and, without taking her shocked eyes from the suave, sophisticated, walking advert for Savile Row, she nervously smoothed out the rucked part with the toe of her short ankle-boot.

'Mr Parry?' she croaked.

He didn't speak. Not a word. Slowly his hand came up and removed the heavy framed glasses from his face and the iron-grey eyes that were revealed were darkly suspicious.

Fran's breath caught in her throat, for without glasses that was the effect the man had on her senses. As if he had the power to draw the air from the room, leaving it eerie and vacuum-like. He wasn't short, balding or old but tall, lean and dark-featured. Mid-thirties, Fran guessed, though the sprinkling of grey in his perfectly groomed black hair confused her.

Fran held his suspicious gaze with rapt curiosity. For all his devastatingly good looks he appeared to be as cold and uninteresting as a sherry trifle minus the sherry. Fran found her thoughts flicking to her sister. Yes, how easy to picture these two as lovers—robot lovers! Not a warm, human passion between them.

'I'm Francyne Cain, Fran for short,' she offered quickly. 'Helena's sister.'

The names that rolled so glibly from her tongue didn't register with him, or if they did he was giving a great show of indifference. It occurred to her that she could be mistaken about his identity—he hadn't said. Maybe he was a minion—but no, this man was no employee. The way he held himself, the way he looked at her as if she were nothing but a blot on the landscape. He had power.

She tried again. 'Helena Cain, your secretary,' she prompted without concealing her sarcasm. 'Well, I'm her sister Fran.'

Without a word he put his glasses back over his eyes and Fran watched the fluid movement with interest. He was like a sleek black panther as he turned away from her and opened a door to a reception-room. He strode across the room, furnished much the same as her own opulent room but more of it, and picked up the phone on the desk by the window.

Fran followed and heard him give instructions not to be disturbed and then he swung to face her, freezing Fran somewhere in the centre of the room.

His features were so grim she felt unreasonably afraid; even though she couldn't see his eyes behind their tinted screen she could feel the mistrust from them boring into her.

'Helena's had an accident and that's why I'm here. She's in hospital . . . not seriously hurt,' she added in a rush so as not to alarm him. Silly, she reprimanded herself, nuclear fall-out wouldn't ruffle *him*. 'I expect she will call you herself later, but when I left her earlier she had been sedated...' Oh, it was all hopeless. The smile faded from Fran's pale lips. 'You don't believe me, do you?' Her voice sounded no more than a whimper.

'Frankly, my dear, no,' he drawled Rhettishly and his voice was as smooth as fine whisky.

Fran looked bleakly at him. He made her feel seven years old and several Orphan Annies rolled into one. She hadn't expected this, not from Helena's boss. Helena's boss, she reminded herself. Her sister's employer-stroke-lover, not hers, so what had she to fear from *him*? That comforting thought gave her courage, and clutching the briefcase even tighter to her chest she took a deep breath.

'And frankly, Mr Parry,' she drawled equally smoothly, 'I don't very much care for your attitude. My sister is lying in a hospital bed worried sick about you. I think it would be politeness on your part to give me the benefit of the doubt and listen to what I have to say without looking down your supercilious nose at me as if the cat had dragged me in!'

The glasses were off again and those cold grey eyes slid back at her with a vengeance. 'You have described yourself very aptly,' he insulted and a dark brow rose insolently. 'How do you expect me to react when you slop in here with a preposterous story about being my secretary's sister?' He smiled then—no, sneered. 'You'd better come up with a better tale than that if you wish to hold my attention longer than the ten seconds I'm prepared to suffer you.'

With that he drew back an immaculately starched white cuff, studied his gold Rolex watch and, while Fran gawped in astonishment, proceeded to count off the seconds—in reverse order!

'Three, two, one, zero.' Not sparing her a glance, he straightened his navy pinstripe suit sleeve over his cuff, perched his spectacles on the end of his autocratic nose, reached for the phone and called hotel security.

For ten seconds Fran had stood stunned—now she exploded with rage. Lunging forward she snatched the phone from his hand, gabbled in French that there had been a terrible mistake, apologised profusely and slammed down the receiver.

For the first time she got a reaction from the man, a twitch at the corner of the mouth, a pulse throbbing at his left temple. He was furious—a controlled fury, which was more than Fran could say for her own.

'Are you crazy?' she blurted, green eyes sparkling wildly. 'Here, this is what I came for.' She tossed the briefcase down on the desk, horrified at her own strength as the flattish leather bag skittered on the highly polished surface and shot itself and a pile of neatly stacked papers to the floor. The flimsy papers tossed and bucked and seemed to take forever to land in an untidy heap.

The papers were covered in columns of numbers and figures and, by the look of Jordan Parry's now ashen features, had once been in numerical order.

'I'm sorry.' Her heart thudded at the look on his face. Instinctively she darted to the heap on the floor; unfortunately for them both Parry had the same idea. There was an embarrassing clash of heads and shoulders and Jordan Parry's glasses went askew on his nose. Jerkily he stood up, wrenched at the offending spectacles, threw them down on the desk and raked his fingers through his hair in exasperation.

It was all too much for Fran. She stood up but her legs were weak, and a bubble of hysteria rose in her throat at the sight of Jordan Parry's sophisticated reserve slipping away.

'I'm so sorry,' she began but had to bite her lip to squash the laughter that hovered so dangerously near. She squatted again and retrieved the briefcase with one hand and tried to gather up the papers with the other.

'Leave them!' he bellowed and Fran shot to attention. Wow, she thought, the man isn't a robot after all, he has a temper. For some reason he went up a notch in her estimation.

'I'm really very sorry——'

'And stop bloody apologising!'

Fran took away the notch for bad language. He snatched the briefcase from her hand and she watched as he checked out the contents. The boxed disks were turned over several times and the wadge of paperwork briefly flicked through. Then he replaced them all in the case and pushed it into the top drawer of the desk. He locked it, checked the drawer was secure and slipped the small gold key into the pocket of his matching pinstripe waistcoat. Then he did something that really surprised Fran. He strode across the room to the mini-bar, poured himself a large Scotch and swallowed it in one, as if... as if he badly needed it.

Fran shifted her feet uncomfortably. She was shaken by what she had just seen. Though Helena had emphasised the importance of the disks, Fran had put her dramatics down to her romantic involvement with her boss. Now she realised her mistake. Those disks *were* important. She felt a sudden urge of pride for getting the briefcase safely to him.

'How did that briefcase come to be in your possession?' he asked gravely.

Fran's pride collapsed. *Still* he didn't believe her.

'I've already told you. If you don't believe me then the problem is yours, not mine!' she retorted hotly, watching his eyes turn from suspicious grey to disbelieving black. 'I didn't steal it, if that's what you're thinking. I'd hardly steal from my own sister and fly out here to hand you your own property, now would I? And all the disks are there, five, you've checked them.'

Slowly he circled the desk to stand before her. Fran stiffened at the nearness of him. His face was suddenly different. Alive, aggressive, jaw muscles clenching in anger. Metallic eyes lashed over her now flushed face, settled on her eyes and plunged their virescent depths.

'I don't know what's on those disks yet, do I?' His voice was only marginally short of a snarl. 'Could be a damn Star Wars game for all I know!'

With practice the man could have a sense of humour, Fran thought briefly before jumping at his throat. 'Are you accusing me of swapping those disks?' she shrieked, thoroughly fed up with his crazy accusations.

His expression softened into disdain, as if she were an undesirable cat's hair on his pristine suit. He shook his head doubtfully. 'No, you're too young and dumb to be involved in industrial espionage, but someone must have put you up to this...'

'Industrial espionage!' Fran spluttered, not sure whether to be flattered or not. 'You're mad, do you know that? And you're the dumb one if you ask me. No one has put me up to anything, and if they had I'd hardly be here taking flak from you, would I?'

Uncertainty flickered for a second in his eyes, then they hardened and more accusations came forth. 'You have a point, but there again I have a shrewd suspicion you might be brighter than you appear, Miss Whatever-your-name-is...'

Fran seethed at that and took a step back.

'And don't move away from me when I'm speaking to you,' he growled. 'Perhaps you thought that by coming here and flashing those fascinating eyes at me I might be persuaded to part with even more valuable information.'

There was a no mistaking what he meant and Fran suppressed a gasp of shock at this latest charge. Jordan Parry was paranoid—and then she saw the funny side of it all. This impressive man actually believed that little Fran Cain was capable of working her feminine wiles on him for company secrets.

She laughed disbelievingly. 'You think I'm here to seduce your precious formulas from you, don't you?'

'Aren't you?' he grated.

'Huh! You are a pompous, arrogant fool, Mr Jordan Parry!' Heavens, Helena would kill her for this. 'And I think you need a shot of your own hormones—you're beginning to sound suspiciously like Mata Hari!' With that she spun on her heel to head for the door, but she got nowhere. A powerful arm hauled her back to face him, only closer this time, so close she could smell the Scotch on his warm breath and it was shocking. Shocking because it wasn't at all unpleasant. His next remark was, though.

'You couldn't seduce Casanova if he was strapped to your bedpost and hadn't seen a woman for a month!' he ripped out with such vengeance Fran quaked inside. 'You know far too much about the contents of that briefcase for your own good.'

He meant her mention of the hormones, and Fran wished with all her heart Helena hadn't said anything, wished that Helena hadn't stepped off that kerb... His hands were holding her shoulders quite firmly, but Fran made no attempt to struggle away—why, she couldn't imagine. His power simply transfixed her and she could do nothing about it. Their eyes were locked in unspoken battle. She stared back at him helplessly, waiting for him to say something, anything, even another accusation would release her from this crushing feeling in her chest.

She wasn't afraid though; no, fear was not one of the emotions coursing through her. She caught her own reflection in the mirror of his eyes, saw determination not to be cowed by this impressive man, saw something else she didn't understand.

He must have seen that look too for his grip loosened, fractionally. To Fran it felt more like a caress and her turmoiled thoughts switched to her sister Helena.

She saw them in each other's arms, felt a strange pain stab through her. Her beautiful sister and this devastating man. In spite of all that had happened since she had met him she could see the attraction he held for women. He was aloof, a challenge. He had hidden passion, his virulent anger proved that. How tempting to push that fury to its limits... She stemmed the wicked thoughts, channelled them in Helena's direction, and then her whole body stiffened in rebellion.

This man was Helena's lover, and yet he had shown no concern when Fran had told him she was in hospital. True, he didn't believe she was Helena's sister, but he had been expecting his secretary and surely by now he must realise something was amiss. But no, he was as cold as a fish, and though Fran knew she should hate him for this, she didn't.

She couldn't analyse why she should feel the way she did—oddly relieved that Jordan Parry didn't feel as strongly for her sister as Helena did for him. But what she could analyse and put into cold perspective was that the man *was* a special sort of man, a dangerously special sort of man.

CHAPTER TWO

'IF YOU'RE referring to my mention of the hormones,' Fran blurted at last, not able to bear the suffocating silence any longer, 'Helena told me the disks contained test results of a hormone drug and that's *all* she told me. I know nothing more, I assure you.' She glanced sideways at Jordan Parry's hands still resting on her shoulders. 'Now take your hands off me or it will be my turn to scream for hotel security.'

He let her go and to her disgust Fran realised she was trembling. She glowered at him through thick lashes and the atmosphere between them was as cold and thin as vichyssoise. Abruptly he turned away from her to the bar.

Fran wasn't sure what to do. Turn and walk out, or try to reason with him? But what for? He had his precious disks, didn't he? She opted for her first thought, but had hardly taken two paces across the room when he ordered her back.

'You're going nowhere till you've done some explaining.'

She spun to face him but already he had his back to her. Fran studied him. His hair was bluish black under the light from the crystal chandelier above his head. His back was broad and his hips, concealed by his suit jacket, looked as if they might be narrow. Men in suits confused Fran—they were like beards, they masked and shielded the real man beneath. She wondered what the real Jordan Parry was like, or maybe this *was* him, this rude, arrogant man who expected everyone to jump when he called.

'I *am* Helena's sister,' she told him quietly. 'And she *has* had an accident. She told me how urgently you needed those disks for your conference and she wanted me to bring them. Frankly I wish she hadn't asked me. I wasn't prepared for being accused of lying...' Her voice shook and she stopped. Parry was quick to pick up on her change of tone and turned to her. To cover her embarrassment she swallowed hard and forced out sharply, 'I've done you an enormous favour coming here. The world doesn't revolve around Parry Pharmaceuticals, you know. I've taken time off from my own job and a thank-you wouldn't go amiss!'

She didn't get one, but he offered her a drink and added, 'You'd better sit down before you fall down. You're looking a little pale.'

Pale! Was it any wonder? She sank gratefully into the nearest chair. At least the tremor in her voice had made him realise that this was no way to treat a lady. Gazing glumly at her jeans-clad knees she wished she'd changed before coming to his suite. She didn't look at all like a lady. Jeans didn't command respect.

'What would you like to drink?' he repeated.

She turned her head in his direction. 'Oh, sorry. I'd...I'd like a spritzer, please.'

'And what's that when it's at home?' He looked suspicious and that twitch was at the corner of his mouth again. Was it anger, impatience? She wasn't sure.

'It's not a Molotov cocktail if that's what you're thinking!' she snapped back at him and instantly regretted her sharpness. His eyes lightened in surprise and Fran let out an exhausted sigh. 'I'm sorry, but it's not every day I get accused of industrial espionage. It's white wine with a good swish of Perrier. I find it the only way to take French wine.'

'You don't like French wine?' He looked at her as if she were slightly mad.

Fran felt a flush rise to her cheeks. Sometimes her honesty led her into deep waters. She didn't want a controversial discussion on her taste in wines. She wished she'd plumped for a simple orange juice.

'I think I'm too young to value it. Like good wine, the taste for it appreciates with age. I'm not ready for it yet.'

A dark brow rose at her reply. 'Perhaps you would prefer a German hock, it's probably more suited to an immature palate.'

She wasn't sure if he was mocking her or not, but she let it pass. 'Yes, please. That would be nice.'

'Neat?'

He *was* mocking her. She nodded, and anger pricked at her as she watched him pour the drinks. Her wine and his Scotch. He really did think she wasn't very bright. She wasn't about to let this latest insult pass.

She took the glass he offered and waited till he sat down across from her, a glass-topped coffee-table, at odds with the rest of the décor, coldly separating them.

'I might have an immature palate, Mr Parry, but there is nothing wrong with my brain. I do know the difference between a Mosel and a hock.' She put the untouched wine glass down on the coffee-table. She was about to get up but his quick apology stopped her.

'I'm sorry.' He stood up and reached for her glass. 'I do apologise. I've opened the wrong bottle. To be honest, my mind is elsewhere.'

'Look, it doesn't matter.' She wished she hadn't mentioned it because she could tell he was telling the truth. He did look far-away. 'I like Mosel as well,' she said hurriedly. 'I just thought . . . It doesn't matter.' She was about to say she had thought he was making a fool of her, but she'd said enough already.

He sat down again. 'You're obviously a wine expert.' He smiled for the very first time and his teeth were as white and even and near perfect as she imagined they would be.

She shook her head and as always answered honestly. 'Not at all. In the evenings I work in a wine bar and I know that hock doesn't come out of a green bottle.' She nodded towards the bottle on the bar.

He laughed then and Fran felt a dull thud in the region of her stomach. When he smiled, when he laughed, he was even more devastating. Lucky Helena. Fran sipped her wine. What was she thinking, lucky Helena? I bet he's a Tartar to work for, she mused, but no doubt the after-hours Helena so often put in made up for it. She went hot at the thought.

She lowered her eyes because he was staring at her, and as if guessing who she was thinking of he said, 'I was never aware that Helena had a sister, but now that I look at you more closely I see a slight resemblance around the eyes—the shape, not the colour. Hers are hazel, yours a deep green, both beautifully almond-shaped.'

Unaccustomed to compliments, Fran wasn't sure how to handle this one till she realised that it wasn't a compliment directed at her but at her lovely sister. She smiled in resignation.

'We aren't very alike in looks or nature. I suppose it's the age difference. Helena is fourteen years older than I. I was only three when she left home, so I hardly know her really. I've been living with her for six months now and still don't know her very well. I seem to irritate her for some reason,' she confessed, wondering why she was telling him all this as if he were her family doctor and she wanted a prescription to get on with her sister.

'Why do you live with her, then?'

He didn't know. Somehow she wasn't unduly surprised. Helena had always been one to keep herself to herself and that appeared to go for her lovers too. She might be having an affair with this man but it didn't mean she was close to him. Helena obviously hadn't told him that their father had died and she had taken in her kid sister to save her being turned out into the streets.

'I had nowhere else to go after my father died,' she admitted. 'The house we lived in was rented. I looked after my sick father for two years and I didn't have a job. I couldn't pay the rent after he died, and besides, the landlord wanted to sell the place. Helena suggested I come to London to stay with her till I got on my feet.'

She thought that must have been the first lie she had told in her life. Helena had suggested nothing of the sort. Truth was, Fran had been at the end of her tether and begged to come to London. Her father had suffered during his illness and Fran had been his whipping-boy; his death had been sad but, when Fran faced the truth, a blessed release. For two years she had struggled with her father and Helena had turned a deaf ear to her pleas for help. She had a career and a life and, as she had tritely put it to Fran, helping an aged parent wasn't part of it!

Fran had given up college and her prospects of a career of her own because of her sister's selfishness, but she wasn't bitter. Helena had a beautiful Regency-style home, a career that she adored, money in plenty—yet happiness eluded her. She was still the hard, sour sister Fran remembered from her infrequent duty calls to the terraced cottage in Sussex. She hadn't even cried at their mother's funeral, Fran recalled. Jealousy, her father had explained when Fran had dared to ask why Helena was the way she was. For fourteen years she had been cosseted as an only child and then Fran had arrived late in her parents' life. The early teens were a crucial time in any girl's life, and Helena had taken this sudden switch of her parents' affection to the new baby badly. She'd stuck it out for three years and then she had been off to seek her fortune. Fran knew and understood and had tried so hard to win Helena's affection, but it was an uphill struggle and a situation that was none of her own doing. She blamed her parents for being so fickle with their love. They should have realised how

Helena was suffering. They had failed her miserably.

'Do you have a daytime job as well, or is it just the wine bar?'

Jerked back to the present, Fran stared at him. Suddenly she felt very defensive for her sister. In spite of Helena's failings she cared about this man. He showed no such feelings for her.

'I would have thought you might be more concerned with my sister's well-being than what I do for a living,' she stated stiffly.

His eyes narrowed warningly. It was obvious people didn't speak to Jordan Parry this way.

'You said Helena is in hospital and, whatever is wrong with her, she is no doubt getting the best of attention. Should I be unduly concerned?' he asked smoothly.

His cold callousness shocked her and she spoke out angrily. 'I just thought that her devoted service to Parry Pharmaceuticals might count for something, might arouse a spark of interest in you. But after spending this short time in your company I've come to realise you haven't an iota of anything remotely like humanity in you!' She was on her feet now, sick at the thought that Helena cared for this awful man. 'You have your five floppies, Mr Jordan Parry, and I hope the six of you will be very happy!'

She tried to move, desperate to get out of his presence, but her legs were trapped. The coffee-table had mysteriously jammed against her shins. The toe of Parry's highly polished shoe was responsible.

'Let me out of here!' she fumed. 'You are being very childish!'

'Sit down! I haven't dismissed you yet,' was the cool command that had Fran's anger bubbling.

'Dismissed me! Who are you to dismiss *me*?' She gave the glass table an almighty shove with her legs and it took him completely by surprise. He winced with pain as the edge of the table bit into *his* shin.

'My God, you're a wretch!' he exclaimed, rubbing his leg.

'It's all you deserve for being so unfeeling in your attitude to my sister's accident. What she sees in you I'll never know,' she retaliated, her green eyes flashing brightly.

He stood up to face her, ran an anguished hand through his hair. 'Look, I'm sorry about Helena, but I'm trying to be realistic, not emotional. At this moment in time I'm more concerned for my company and the jobs of two thousand employees——'

'I don't see what that has to do with banal questions about what I do for a living!' she interrupted indignantly.

'Because Helena has left me without her services for this conference, that's why,' he grated back at her as if she should have reasoned that out for herself. 'I asked you what other job you had because if you were capable of a bit of accurate shorthand and typing you could be of some help to me. I don't suppose you can use a computer?'

A fine red mist swam before Fran's eyes and her voice came out in a staccato gasp. 'You mean—you mean...you want me to take Helena's place?'

'That would be absurd,' he snapped, 'no one could take Helena's place, but——'

'Too damn right!' Fran exploded. 'You've got to be out of your mind, Mr Parry! I wouldn't help you out if you were dying of thirst in the Sahara and I was a glass of water. You are insufferable, do you know that? Insufferable! My sister is lying injured in hospital and worried sick about you and you don't care a shirt button for her. She walked in front of a motorbike because she was exhausted after working all night on your silly, silly floppy things... Oh, *you*!'

She flung out of the suite and this time he didn't stop her. Blindly she tore along the corridor back to her room. She bombed straight into the bathroom to splash cool water on her face. He'd made her so angry she had wanted to hit him— if she'd been a man she would have done! She dabbed her burning cheeks dry with a towel. How could a man so...so attractive be so perfectly horrible?'

He was standing by the window when she came out of the bathroom, studying her sketch and comparing it with the boulevard scene below. Fran's heart pumped as she stopped dead in the middle of her bedroom and saw him. He didn't turn to her, didn't speak, just stood leaning on the window-frame, thoughtfully staring at her sketch.

His tie was loose round his collar now and a strand of dark hair lay out of place on his forehead. His face looked different, somehow softer, as if the fight had gone out of him.

Her first impulse was to snatch her pad from his fingers and order him out of her room, but that would be childish and Fran was feeling far from childish. A strange sensation crackled down her spine and she was strongly aware of an atmosphere in the warm room, something that couldn't be explained, something she didn't quite understand but felt, deep inside her.

Paris, this hotel, this bedroom, this man. Fran bit her lip. She had never experienced anything like this before but nevertheless some feminine instinct told her what it was. Tension, a strong sexual tension that made the air thick and heavy. But he was a man of substance and power and she was barely a woman, not in age, but in experience of life and yet, uncannily, she was able to recognise the atmosphere for what it was.

He turned his head towards her and his eyes held hers for what seemed like eternity. And then he spoke in a voice that was thick and throaty.

'You make me feel alive,' he said slowly.

The air was charged with undercurrents of such fierce intensity that Fran's legs nearly went from under her. She couldn't hold his gaze but looked away. She had seen vulnerability in the soft grey of his eyes, a vulnerability she wouldn't have believed possible from the sophisticated image he gave out. She didn't want to see any more. She moved to the dressing-table, shifted the lamp an inch and shifted it back again.

'Do I make you feel that way because I shout at you and answer you back?' she asked him huskily.

'Possibly,' he murmured.

'You're not used to that, are you? You command respect and subservience.'

'I don't command it but my position decrees it.'

'Am I supposed to feel sorry for you?' She lifted her chin and looked at him. No, it wasn't pity he was looking for, but she read something else in his eyes. A need, a dangerous need. Then the look was gone and the polyurethane scratch-resistance was back.

'Let's stop this conversation before it gets out of hand,' he said coolly. He tossed her pad down on the bed and came across to her. 'I was serious about you helping me out. Give yourself a scrub,' he reached out and pulled the tatty ribbon from her hair, 'and do something with this and you could look quite respectable.'

She refused to rise to his insult and lash back. He enjoyed goading her, actually got a kick out of it. Well, she wasn't here to pleasure him, in any way.

'I can't do anything for you, Mr Parry,' she told him calmly. 'I'm not a secretary and I'm not a punch-bag either, so take your grievances out on someone else. You have the information you want for your conference tomorrow——' she held his gaze purposely, cool green eyes loaded with double meaning '—*that's* as far as my services go.'

She crossed to the bed and gathered up her sketch-pad and shoulder-bag. Her holdall was by the bed where she had dumped it earlier. She hadn't even unpacked and now she was on the move again. Mission accomplished.

'What are you doing?' he asked quietly.

'Leaving, of course. I've delivered your disks and now I'm going.' She said it offhandedly, as if she didn't care if she never saw him again, but the horror was she did. He infuriated her, insulted her and yet he excited her. She squeezed her eyes tightly, to somehow try and see the world clearly. What was happening to her?

'You won't get a flight at his hour.'

'Who said anything about a flight?' she retorted, lifting her holdall. 'I'm booking out of the Clermont, not out of Paris. I'll find another hotel.' She hoped she sounded very independent and streetwise, but secretly she was quaking at the thought of tramping the wet streets in the dark looking for a hotel she could afford.

'And how far do you think you'll get without money?'

She thumped her bag down on the carpet again and with hands on narrow hips defied him across the room. 'I'm quite solvent, thank you very much.' She had a credit card and some cash. It was enough.

'And your return flight ticket?'

The interrogative way he was firing these questions suggested that he wasn't worried about her welfare but more concerned by the company expense account. She gave him a wan smile. 'Yes, I do have a return flight ticket, and before you say any more Helena paid for it on her own Amex, not Parry Pharmaceuticals' account. So if you have any funny ideas about confiscating my ticket, forget them!' Heavens, what was she saying? She was implying he was trying to stop her leaving, which was crazy of course.

'So you plan to fly back to London tomorrow?'

There was something in his voice that told her her suspicions weren't unfounded. He sounded almost smug and looked dangerously sure of himself. He was leaning on the dressing-table, hands plunged into his trouser pockets, one leg crossed over the other. For the first time she noticed a thread of burgundy through the navy pinstripe suit and thought what an odd thing to think of at a time like this.

'Tomorrow afternoon.'

'You have a passport?'

Fran sighed wearily. He was asking the most absurd things. She bent and picked up her bags. 'How do you think I got here if I didn't have...?' She let go of the bags and gave out a mournful groan. Of course, she saw it all now. 'My passport, my money. They are all in Helena's briefcase, aren't they?'

She'd forgotten she'd put them there for safe-keeping. Helena had made her promise to guard the bag with her life, and as it had been clutched to Fran's chest for most of the journey it had seemed the sensible place to put her own valuables. Now it was in an even safer place— Jordan Parry's locked desk drawer.

'You are going to give them back to me, aren't you?' she asked in a small voice.

'I have no such intention,' he told her crisply.

'But why?' Fran breathed anxiously, her eyes nervously searching his features for some sort of answer. Surely he wasn't serious about her helping him during the conference? And surely she had been mistaken about the other need she imagined she had seen in his eyes?

He didn't seem to think her question warranted an answer, just stood there looking at her, his grey eyes unreadable now.

She gave a dismissive shrug of her shoulders. 'It's really no problem. I shall go to the British Consulate and tell them you've stolen my things. They'll soon sort you out.'

'The consulate is a long way from here and it's pouring with rain.'

'I'll get the Metro, I've got a *carnet*...' She hadn't. It was in the briefcase, everything was in the briefcase. She hadn't a franc to her name.

He started to move towards her and Fran thought that any second he would be in striking distance and she might hit him. Her small fists clenched at her sides. She wouldn't, she couldn't—even a slap would mean physical contact and she must avoid that at all costs.

'Where do we go from here?' she croaked out in desperation.

A sardonic smile slicked his face. 'I intend to employ you for a week or so.' His hand came up and twisted a tendril of her blonde hair between his finger and thumb. Fran flinched. 'Tame this. Have you any decent evening wear with you? No matter if you haven't. I'm sure we can sort something out. I need you for the duration of this conference. You have no choice but to accept my conditions.'

'C . . . conditions?' she squeaked.

'I'll pay you for your work, generously. Your accommodation at the Clermont goes without saying. You will have plenty of free time to pursue your hobby,' his eyes acknowledged her sketch-pad on the bed, 'and when I've finished with you I'll return your passport and make sure you are safely returned home.'

Fran felt the edge of the dressing-table biting into the backs of her thighs. How had they got here? He was almost pinning her against it.

'I . . . I can be of no use to you, Mr Parry,' she husked. 'I can't type . . . I . . . can't . . .'

'You can do a lot for me, Fran Cain,' his voice grazed. He was so close Fran felt his warmth, his smell. She thought he was about to kiss her and fear welled inside her. If he did that she would be lost, she knew it. And then he moved away from her, so abruptly she felt a wave of icy loss.

'But before we seal our agreement I would like to apologise to you.' He stood by the window again and Fran's head buzzed. Seal our agreement—apologise!

'What do you mean?' Fran uttered weakly. She sat down on the dressing-table stool, her legs no longer able to support her. Was it possible to suffer jet lag from London to Paris? Her head was spinning.

His apology, soft-timbred, floated on the air. 'I'm sorry if I've appeared cold and unfeeling. I do care about Helena's welfare and I know her well enough to know that whatever has happened she is coping. Helena has been very supportive over these last troubled months and I really do appreciate all she has done for the company. She may or may not have told you the company is attempting a take-over. It entails a lot of work and stress. It's catching up on me and I'm sorry if I was unpleasant to you. I was expecting her and not you in my suite. It was a shock to find a slip of a girl, in jeans and a sweater several sizes too big for her, passing herself off as my secretary's sister.'

'I *am* her sister,' Fran protested. 'And I'm not a slip of a girl—I'm twenty-two!'

He smiled then. 'Well, act it and hear me out.' Fran bit her lip and looked away. 'Thank you for bringing the briefcase to me. Its contents are of enormous value to me. I'm about to launch a new drug that will put us in an even stronger bargaining position to gain control of Unimet. I'm sure you can be of further assistance to me.'

Fran shook her head dismally. 'I don't see how, I really don't.' She walked slowly towards him at the window. 'I've already told you I'm not a secretary.' She stopped at the other side of the window, gazed down at the street below. It was quieter now, the commuters home. The rain had ceased. 'I'm not Helena,' she added softly.

'No, you're not Helena,' he whispered.

'You're not used to apologising, are you?'

'I don't usually have to.'

'You were very rude to me,' she murmured.

'I know. It was uncalled for.' A pause before he went on. 'Will you stay and help me?'

How strange he was, Fran mused. One minute an ogre, the next... Helena couldn't have stood a chance with him, he could be so persuasive. But as they had both agreed she wasn't a Helena, and she wasn't about to fall into his arms and dance to his tune, tempting though it was. She would have to be firm.

'I work in an art gallery during the day and a wine bar at night—hardly conducive to selling drugs, is it?' was the only fight she could put up.

He looked across to her and smiled. 'It sounds perfect to me.'

She frowned in puzzlement. 'What do you mean?'

'You're beautiful, you speak French fluently, you know about art and wine...'

'And nothing about your company,' she added, refusing to acknowledge his compliments.

'You don't need to know anything. I want a hostess, not a sales rep.'

'A hostess!' Fran gasped, her mind whirling crazily. 'And what does that entail exactly? Fishnet tights, a basque and a whip?'

To her surprise he grinned widely. 'Sounds very interesting, but not exactly what I had in mind. Seminars like this are not all lectures and medical jargon. There's a lot of socialising as well. It's all a part of the accepted set-up. Wine and dine the clients, mostly eminent consultants, and subtly convince them they can't practise without my products.'

'I fail to see where I fit in.'

'I need an attractive woman at my side to add a little light relief after the pressures of the lectures. The consultants bring their wives with them and in the evenings there will be cocktail parties and dinners. I need someone...'

'To hand round the canapés,' Fran finished for him.

His enigmatic smile was beginning to be a habit. 'Something like that,' he said.

A police car, sirens screaming, whooshed down the boulevard. Fran was glad of the diversion away from her jumbled thoughts. He'd tried to make it all sound so glamorous—wining and dining with the medical fraternity—but what it amounted to was her handing round soggy canapés and topping up their drinks. A glorified waitress.

Would he really keep her money and passport? she pondered as she watched with mild interest the gendarmes swarming into a restaurant across the road. It was nothing short of blackmail and yet his offer of her accommodation and free time to explore Paris was so tempting. If he was that ageing martinet with the bald head she would almost certainly have agreed, but he wasn't. He was this man standing next to her, this Jordan Parry who was far too good-looking for her good. She smiled inwardly. How stupidly and naïvely she was thinking. He couldn't possibly be interested in anything more than employing her. He had Helena, and though Fran didn't have a low opinion of herself she was sensible enough to acknowledge that, for Jordan Parry, Helena was his sort of woman.

'I'll have to think about your offer, Mr Parry,' she said after the gendarmes had emerged from the restaurant with a struggling chef who looked a little the worse for drink. 'But if I don't agree you will give me back my things, won't you?'

'I've already told you I have no such intention. What can I do or say to make you think otherwise?' He stepped towards her, his grey eyes suddenly dancing with mischief.

Momentarily shocked by this sudden new expression on his face, she parted her lips in surprise. His forefinger came up under her chin and tilted it. His mouth came down on hers so swiftly her breath caught in her throat. She held it as his lips softened against hers. His arm slid around her waist and gently eased her closer to him. The length of his body was pressed against hers, not fiercely but gently as if not to hurt her. She felt weak and woozy as her senses noted the delicious pressure of his mouth on hers, the muzzy scent of an exclusive cologne. His breathing was imperceptible; hers came in a rush as he drew away from her.

'I'll give you twenty minutes,' he murmured throatily.

'Twenty minutes of what?' she uttered stupidly.

He laughed softly. 'How quaint you are! I'll give you twenty minutes to get ready for dinner. Do you have any other clothes with you?'

She nodded.

'Good. I'll meet you in Reception in twenty minutes.'

He left her standing at the window and she didn't move till she heard the firm click of the door closing behind him. Then in a daze she went to the bathroom, gazed in the mirror and gingerly touched her hot, sensitive lips. She had thought him a cold, unfeeling animal but he had kissed her as she had never been kissed before. With warmth, not passion or need but warmth, almost as if he didn't want to scare her and frighten her off. She was afraid though. She was afraid of him, of Helena, of herself. A man who kissed like that...

CHAPTER THREE

So why was she getting ready to have dinner with Jordan? Fran asked herself several times as she scooted around, shampooing and preening till she glowed and tingled with radiant life. Wasn't she playing with fire? It was the thought of her sister that quelled that thought. She was no match for Helena and her sophistication. To Jordan Parry the kiss and the dinner invitation were just an extension of his apology. He had mistreated her and was making up for it. The crazy sexual tension she had imagined she had felt earlier was her starved imagination working overtime.

Never mind, she mused as she blow-dried her golden hair, she could fantasise, couldn't she? Imagine that he had asked her out because he had wanted to. He had admitted she made him feel alive; maybe he fancied a bit more of that treatment over dinner, repartee with someone who didn't think him God's gift to the world as Helena did. It would make a change for him.

She was glad she'd had the foresight to pack her only decent dress. A very understated black fine wool dress that Helena had been surprised she had purchased.

'Hardly your style at all, dear,' she had sniffed.

'I wonder what my style is,' Fran had bit back sarcastically. 'I've hardly had a bash at life yet to find out what suits me best.'

Helena had huffed off out for the evening after that, leaving Fran with her night off to regret being so spiteful. But she couldn't help it sometimes. Whatever Fran did or said her sister would put her down in some way or another.

As Fran twirled in front of the mirror at the Clermont she thought Helena would probably not approve of her now. Her long hair gleamed gold and wisped seductively around her oval-shaped face. Her lips, full and glossed a delicate peach colour, were a perfect complement to her sea-green eyes with their fringing of thick dark lashes. Golden hair and dark lashes—a quirk of nature which annoyed Fran at times. People were wrongly inclined to presume she dyed one or the other. Jordan Parry had thought her eyes fascinating. Fran shivered at the reminder and fixed baby pearl studs in the lobes of her ears.

And the dress—well, that certainly wasn't her usual casual mode of dress, she had to admit. It clung to her slender figure for grim death. Fran stood back from the mirror. Her new black patent high heels were agony and made her legs look endlessly long, but apart from that she had to admit she felt OK.

She couldn't see Jordan in Reception and wondered if he'd had second thoughts, or even forgotten about her. She perched herself on the

edge of a burgundy leather chesterfield and
waited, smiling to herself, thinking that six
months ago, before coming to London, she would
have fled the admiring looks she was getting from
the multinational guests at the hotel. Before the
art gallery and the wine bar, she had been nothing
more than a country mouse. But London life had
knocked her rural timidity from her in next to
no time. She was far from Helena's confident
level, but men giving her admiring glances didn't
bother her—there was plenty of that in the wine
bar. She had learnt to pass off the constant
requests for dates with a pleasant smile and a little
joke that left no one offended.

Fran tried not to fidget on the seat but she was
a little anxious now. It was more than twenty-
five minutes since... And then she saw him as
the lift gates opened. He stood politely back to
let an older woman out before him. The woman
gave him an appreciative smile and her eyes
lingered hungrily. Fran understood why. He
looked superb in a black evening suit. A black
overcoat, probably cashmere by the fall of it,
hung cape-fashion from his broad shoulders. A
vampire count, Fran thought, her neck tingling.

She thanked God for the little black dress and
the smart shoes that were squeezing the life blood
from her toes. The agony was worth it to be seen
in his company, and she wouldn't let him down.
She rose gracefully to her feet and waited for him
to spot her, which surely he would because he

was heading her way. She planted a smile of greeting on her slightly flushed face and waited.

'Oh, no,' she muttered under her breath. Without his glasses he hadn't seen her, walked straight past as if she were a stick of furniture. She called out in a hushed whisper, 'Mr Parry! Mr Parry! You didn't recognise me, did you?' She tugged at his sleeve and when he turned she gave him a wide smile.

His face was a picture of astonishment and then he smiled, his eyes flicking over her in approval. 'You're very right. I didn't recognise you.'

'You would have done if you had worn your glasses,' she cajoled lightly. 'There's nothing to be ashamed of in wearing glasses, you know.' She matched his step as he took her elbow and guided her towards the front of the hotel.

'They are a recent acquisition, and I only wear them for reading; I didn't recognise you because I was looking for a little wretch, not...' He glanced at her sideways, still not sure if his eyes were deceiving him or not.

'Not what?' Fran prompted, eager for the compliment she felt sure was on the tip of his tongue.

'Not anything,' he sighed resignedly. 'I can't think of a suitable adjective to describe the transformation.'

'How about amazing?' she suggested.

'You're not very modest, are you?'

'Not when I know the metamorphosis is a minor miracle. I looked a mess when I arrived in your suite. I did my best for you tonight by way of saying I'm sorry.'

He smiled. 'Thank you for being so thoughtful.' There was a slight twinkle in his eye.

'Where are we going?' she asked uncertainly as he ushered her through the revolving doors of the hotel, down the steps and into the back of a chauffeur-driven car.

'To an intimate little restaurant I know by the river,' he informed her, settling next to her, so close she had to inch away.

'Oh, I thought we would be eating in the hotel restaurant,' she said uneasily. She hadn't anticipated this! An intimate restaurant! The hotel would be much safer, surely?

Fran sank back into the luxurious leather upholstery and gazed mournfully out of the window at the dark, tree-lined boulevards they were skimming down. The whole idea of staying to help him with his socialising suddenly palled. She doubted if she'd get through this first evening with him without making some sort of gigantic *faux pas*. Fran shivered, wishing she hadn't come.

'You're cold.' He tucked a tartan travel-rug round her knees.

'Thank you,' she murmured, then, 'Why on earth do you want me to help you out with your socialising? I'll only let you down, you know. I'll drop the vol-au-vents and spill the wine. I'll make silly remarks at the wrong moment—why, I might even get drunk . . . I might——'

'You might not do anything of the sort,' he cut in confidently.

'Are you prepared to take that risk?'

'I wouldn't have asked you to stay if I didn't think you could handle it.' He turned to her, reached across and smoothed a wisp of fine hair from her cheek. 'You're a very lovely and sharp girl, Fran, don't underestimate yourself.'

He'd used her Christian name and it sang like church bells in Fran's ears. She couldn't look at him, suffered the closeness of him with her body tensed to breaking-point and wished she were back at the hotel taking a sandwich in her room. This night was a mistake. He was too smooth by far.

'I'm not underestimating myself, Mr Parry,' she murmured. 'I just don't think you know what you are doing.'

'I know *exactly* what I am doing,' he said decisively, smoke-grey eyes straight ahead. There was an edge to his tone that had Fran's nerves jangling. He always got his own way, that was for sure, and what was his own way this time?

'I can't stay.' She'd made up her mind. In that instant she knew it would be dangerous. 'There are a million reasons why I can't——'

'Well, I'm afraid I haven't time to hear them all now,' he cut in as the car purred to a halt at the kerbside.

They had stopped outside the restaurant across
from the riverbank. The chauffeur held the door
open for her and Fran stepped out. It was driz-
zling again and a cool breeze ruffled her hair.
She was dreading the evening ahead of her. She
wondered how far a feigned headache would get
her. Too late—Jordan Parry had dismissed his
driver for the evening and the car pulled away.

The restaurant was warm and unashamedly
romantic. Soft lights, soft music and a delicious
pot-pourri of scents greeted them: good cooking
and the heady fragrance of roses at the centre of
the dining tables. It was already crowded with
beautiful people and they were ushered to a
velvety alcove reserved for them. Fran wedged
herself into the corner, no longer wishing she was
back at the hotel with a sandwich but praying
that a small miracle would whisk her back to
London at the blink of an eye.

'Don't look petrified.' Jordan smiled across at
her and Fran smiled back, trying to relax because
her common sense told her she could do nothing
about the situation she had allowed herself to be
so easily led into. But it certainly was unnerving
being out with this man. Every woman's head
had turned as Jordan Parry had walked into the
restaurant. Fran wasn't sure how to react, to lift
her chin with pride or shrink like the little country
mouse she had once been.

She tilted her chin up proudly, and why not?
It wasn't every night you were escorted to an

exclusive Parisian diner with a man as special as this.

'The decorations on these walls are art deco and no cheap reproduction,' she told him, admiring the gold and burgundy mirror across the room.

He smiled as if sensing she was striving for conversation. 'Does that sort of décor appeal to you?' he asked after ordering aperitifs and glancing briefly at the menu.

Fran shook her head, studied the menu and replied, 'I like it but not to live with. When I get a place of my own I shall fill it with wild flowers, hang water-colours of Mediterranean patios on the yellow walls and relax in worn baggy sofas.' She closed the leather-bound menu. 'I'll have the consommé julienne followed by *noisettes d'agneau à la* Clamart.'

'I'll join you in the soup...'

Fran giggled and then bit her lip, for Jordan hadn't realised what he had said.

Then the penny dropped and he grinned with her. 'I'll rephrase that, shall I? I'll have the same soup as you followed by *suprêmes de volaille* Rossini.'

'What's that?' Fran asked, eyes wide with interest.

Jordan studied her with smoky grey eyes before replying. 'How different you are from Helena. She would never be so open and ask such a question.'

It had been a mistake to accept his dinner invitation, Fran thought with regret, and lowered her eyes to the roses on the table. She was gauche and awkward and Helena was sophisticated, but somehow that was nothing to the pain of hearing him mention her sister so casually. How many intimate restaurants like these had he wined and dined Helena in?

'Helena wouldn't need to ask,' Fran told him. 'She'd know.'

'Maybe,' Jordan said smoothly, 'but her pride wouldn't allow her to ask if she didn't. That's why you are so very different.'

Fran glared at him. 'Are you saying I have no pride——?'

His hand closed so reassuringly over hers she felt the flare of embarrassment and temper cool. 'I'm saying nothing of the sort. What I'm trying to say, and not having much success, is that I find your honesty beguiling. You didn't know what it was and you were open enough to ask.'

Her eyelashes fluttered unwillingly. 'It was gauche,' she murmured, slyly trying to draw her fingers out from under his.

He let her, watching as she clenched them in her lap. He shrugged in agreement. 'OK, it was gauche. I like gauche.'

She caught the glimmer of humour in his eyes and relaxed slightly. 'So what is it?' she persisted. Though now, she didn't even want to know what he had ordered. It didn't matter. How could anything matter when her heart was being squeezed so tight in her chest she could hardly draw breath. His touch had been like warm silk, his eyes on hers bewitching. She clenched her fingers tightly to drive away the thoughts that skidded recklessly round her mind. Thoughts of him and her sister.

'Rossini and the French chef Auguste Escoffier were friends. He created this dish in Rossini's honour. Chicken breasts with pâté and a Madeira sauce,' he explained. 'Would you like to change your order?'

She smiled and shook her head. 'It sounds delicious but I'll stick to the lamb.'

'Then you can try it next time,' he told her, leaning back in his seat to allow room for the wine waiter to put down their drinks.

Would there be a next time, Fran wondered bleakly, or was that what people said at such moments? Empty conversation that didn't mean a thing. She glanced at him, disappointed that he was occupied watching a couple leaving. He looked relaxed this evening and Fran would have liked to have flattered herself with the thought that she might be the reason. But it was more than likely he was simply relieved his floppy disks had arrived in time for the conference.

He looked back at her and they both smiled and almost immediately looked away again.

'So tell me more about yourself,' he said, raising a martini to his lips.

Oh, this was awful, Fran thought dismally. Worse than she had anticipated. They were stiff and formal with each other and Helena was like a wedge between them. How could she relax and even attempt to enjoy the evening knowing that if fate hadn't intervened her sister would be sitting across from him now?

She shrugged her narrow shoulders, made an attempt to make the best of a bad mistake. 'You know just about everything. I sell paintings by day, wine by night.'

'Do you have a boyfriend?'

Fran smiled at that. 'Hardly have the time, do I?'

'Why drive yourself so hard?'

'I looked after my sick father for two years.' She raised honest eyes to his. 'I loved him very much but those two years felt like ten.' He nodded as if knowing exactly what she meant. 'I'm making up for that lost time. I'm learning about life and about myself.'

'Do you need two jobs to achieve that?' he asked.

'I also want my independence from Helena,' she admitted, wondering if she should have said that in the circumstances. After all, Helena and this man ... She didn't want to think about it. 'I was at art school before my father's illness, but didn't complete my course. I'm not trained to do anything specific so I thought the best thing to do was to come to London where it's all supposed to be happening.' She grinned ruefully. 'Nothing much has happened yet. I tried to get into commercial art but no one in that sector wants to risk someone untrained and unqualified. I took the two jobs to earn enough for a deposit on a place of my own, a small studio flat where I can paint and think and try and make a new life for myself.'

'I can understand that,' he said quietly.

'Can you?' She frowned, not believing for a minute he could. This man with his wealth and power couldn't possibly understand.

'I gave up my passion for the sake of my father too.'

Fran's eyes widened in astonishment. 'Your passion? What do you mean?'

He leaned back in his seat. 'More a vocation than a passion.' He smiled. 'I was a general practitioner...'

'*Was*! You mean you got struck off?' she croaked in a strangled voice, her mind spinning off at a tangent at the thought of the misdemeanours he had committed to get thrown out of the medical profession.

'What an imagination you have.' He laughed. 'No, I didn't get struck off. I gave it up to go into the family business.'

'You gave up all that training, a vocation in life, to sell drugs?'

'You make it sound as if I ply my trade in a street market.' He smiled at her. His eyes softened sympathetically. 'I understand what you are trying to do. My father had a stroke and couldn't run the company any more. I gave up my work for his. Sometimes you have to make such sacrifices for someone you love. He died last year. Like you, I am free now,' he added poignantly, and held her eyes for a long second.

From then on the evening was easier for Fran. It was a relief to talk about her father with someone who understood her mixed feelings of guilt and remorse and loss. The time sped by smoothly. The food was delicious and the French wine perfect.

'French wine?' Fran laughed in disbelief when Jordan showed her the label. 'Have I been drinking French wine all evening?' He nodded and she murmured, 'I must be growing up.'

And the feelings she had when later he slipped his cashmere coat around her shoulders as they strolled along the banks of the Seine were very grown up. Like Helena, I could fall in love with you, she inwardly teased herself, dallying with the fantasy of being his mistress till it became too desperate to think about.

His arm closed around her shoulders as he guided her round a greasy puddle in the road. They passed the puddle and Jordan's arm remained around her shoulders and Fran wanted time to stand still.

'Are you very tired?' Jordan asked as they stopped on the embankment to gaze across the river. The stars and the moon and street lamps were reflected in the glittering metallic water. Fran memorised the scene to be recalled later on canvas. Jordan's nearness, the warmth of his arm around her, didn't need slotting away in her memory banks; the feeling would be with her forever.

'I was earlier,' she admitted. 'The cool night air has perked me up. What did you have in mind?' she asked openly. Maybe he wanted to go on to a nightclub. The thought catapulted her into fantasy land again. She was in his arms smooching to George Benson...

'I had an appointment earlier on.' He drew his arm tighter around her to look at his watch. 'Missed it now but there's a chance...' He didn't finish. A ragged moan came from somewhere deep in his throat as he looked down at her cocooned in the warmth of his coat, her eyes, upturned to his, wide and silvered in the light from the moon. 'You're so beautiful,' he husked before his mouth closed over hers.

No fantasy this time. Just sweet reality. She had never been kissed like this before, never known such depth of pleasure. Her arms wanted to link around his neck but they were imprisoned at her sides, swathed in his coat. When at last he released her Fran tried in vain to understand the look in his dark eyes.

'Come on, if we hurry we can make it.' He clutched her hand tightly in his and urged her quickly through a network of narrow streets, away from the riverbank and the moon and the stars.

Fran's feeling of loss was immense. She forced laughter as she tried to keep up with him and he laughed too and slowed his pace, but inwardly she was crying. When Jordan had kissed her she hadn't given a thought to Helena, but afterwards, looking up into his eyes, she had seen her sister's face reflected there. Her conscience pulling her up with a short sharp jolt, no doubt. The thought was so dismal.

'Jordan, where are we going?' She'd used his Christian name for the first time and it sounded strange coming from her own lips.

'An art gallery.' He turned to her suddenly. 'A bit of a busman's holiday for you. Do you mind?'

'At this time of night? Won't it be closed?'

'Paris never closes.' He stopped on the corner of a wider boulevard, more brightly lit than the narrower streets they had left behind. 'Fran,' his voice was suddenly leaden with concern, 'you must be tired. Would you rather I took you back to the hotel? This can wait till another day.'

She shook her blonde head vigorously. 'I want to see everything,' she enthused. If she was honest with herself she would admit to exhaustion, but she didn't want the night with him to end. 'Might as well see what the French art opposition are up to.' She smiled.

He squeezed her hand and they crossed the road to the Delphine Gallery.

As soon as they entered the plate glass doors and a reverential silence slipped around them like a clinging mist Fran was lost. The paintings displayed were exquisite and she gasped in delight, her eager green eyes darting over the collection of oils and water-colours.

'Oh, Jordan,' she husked, pulling him towards a delicate water-colour of a run-down apple orchard with a pale, haunting château in the background. 'This is beautiful. You can almost smell the pulpy windfalls on the ground.'

He stood behind her, looking over her shoulder, his hands gently holding her upper arms. His breath when he spoke was warm on the top of her head. 'It's just the sort of painting I'd imagined you would like. It's like you. Warm, delicate and sensual.' His lips brushed the tips of her ears and Fran closed her eyes in ecstasy.

'Jordan! Two hours late but I knew you would come,' came a shrill, excited voice from behind them.

Jordan and Fran turned and in that instant Jordan took his hands from her to embrace a fluttering apparition in scarlet and heliotrope silk.

'Stella, I'm sorry, but we got held up.' He bent his head to kiss both cheeks of the petite, vivacious woman whose eyes sparkled brightly for Jordan but darkened noticeably when Jordan introduced Fran.

Fran held her hand out politely and smiled, and thought that Stella was probably about Helena's age but charged with a fiery effervescence that her sister lacked. They had one thing in common, though, Fran was quick to spot: their attraction to Jordan Parry.

'Delighted to meet you,' Stella simpered, but she wasn't, Fran sensed.

She was beautifully made up, her hair a startling red-gold, she smelled expensive and Fran guessed the effort had been made for Jordan. Why else would her huge golden eyes tarnish so rapidly at the sight of Fran? Fran felt a thrill of power; this exotic woman was wary of her, she had been expecting Jordan on his own. Anger pushed aside that thrill and she was suddenly cross with Jordan for exposing her to this. It made her feel as if she didn't belong.

'Fran, Jordan and I have some business to sort out; perhaps you would like to look at the pictures at the back of the gallery. Much more your style,' Stella suggested brightly.

Shades of Helena, Fran thought miserably as she turned away.

'I'd rather like Fran's opinion on my purchases, Stella,' Jordan stated firmly and Fran's heart leapt. She wanted to hug him for that.

Stella's face was a picture in itself. She glanced at Fran in resigned sufferance and turned into the tiny office behind the gallery. They all squeezed in and Fran saw a bottle of champagne on ice and two glasses on the desk. Again Fran felt a spurt of anger directed at Jordan. He shouldn't have brought her.

The three oils Jordan had purchased from Stella were lovely. Two Provence landscapes and a still life—dried flowers, autumn fruits on a sun-bleached rustic table. They were quite conventional but none the less lovely for that. Fran wasn't unduly surprised by his choice. They were 'safe' purchases, would accrue in value and had a timeless appeal.

'They're lovely, Jordan,' she breathed, sharply aware of Stella scratching around in the filing cabinet for another glass.

'Which house are they for?' Stella asked, pouring the champagne so badly it frothed over the glasses and left pools on the desk. 'Eaton Square, Monte Carlo or...'

Fran left at that point, took her champagne and squeezed out of the tiny office that was made for two. She wandered into the other studio behind the main gallery, and gazed in disgust at the pictures that were supposedly more her style. Hideous abstracts painted in harsh colours and in a frenzied rush.

She could hear the murmur of Jordan's voice, the tinkling laughter from Stella. She felt incredibly alone. Then she heard Jordan thanking Stella for her help, his tone implying their business was over and it was time they left, but Stella insisted they have another drink. Jordan murmured his agreement and Fran felt irritation whisper down her spine.

'I thought you'd like these,' Stella said, coming up to stand next to her, ready to pour the dregs of the bottle of champagne into Fran's glass. Fran moved her glass away in refusal.

'By the look on Fran's face I don't think she does,' Jordan said for her, a mocking glitter to his eyes. Fran seethed inside and gave him a blank look. She was perfectly capable of speaking for herself, given the chance.

Jordan went on to tell Stella that Fran worked in a gallery in London and was herself an accomplished artist. Fran remembered her sketchpad in her bedroom and her heart fluttered at the thought of Jordan leaning by the window, gazing at her drawing. Then her heart took an enormous leap.

Stepping forward across the room, she stopped in front of a square canvas, frowned and let out a gasp of surprise at the abstract.

'This is a Lafarge.'

'You know his work?' Stella asked in surprise.

'Yes, I was at art school with him,' Fran breathed incredulously. 'I knew him well. His brother died tragically in a boating accident in the South of France and he left England quickly. We lost touch.'

She stared at the dull canvas, only just recognisable as Jean-Claude's work. He used to paint so vibrantly but this work was a mere shadow of

the artist she once knew. She wondered how badly
the loss of his brother had affected his life—it
had certainly affected his work.

'I've sold several of his canvases. In fact I'm
picking up more tomorrow. Why don't you come
with me?' came the surprising suggestion from
Stella.

Stunned by this sudden show of warmth, Fran
swung and faced her.

'Oh, I couldn't...' She looked to Jordan for
support but there was nothing forthcoming from
him. His eyes were expressionless.

'Jordan tells me you are helping out at his little
conference but surely he can spare you for a few
hours? I could pick you up at the hotel.' Stella
smiled sweetly at Jordan then and Fran suddenly
understood what was going on. Their business
transactions were over but Stella had no intention
of letting Jordan go. She was quite prepared to
use Fran to get to him.

'No, I don't think——'

'Nonsense! I'll call you in the morning to
arrange a time.'

In desperation Fran turned to Jordan,
expecting a protest, but all she saw was a tight-
ening of his jaw. Couldn't he see she didn't want
to get involved with Stella or her old artist friend?
Fran bit the inside of her lip. Of course he
couldn't see, because he didn't care. For a few
instants tonight she had thought... Was she out

of her mind? Jordan didn't care a flea's eyebrow for her!

'Well, if Jordan doesn't object,' her green eyes defied him to now, 'I'd be delighted to join you and look dear Jean-Claude up after all this time.' Her tone matched the defiance of her gaze.

'So Miss Wide-Eyed Innocence has a skeleton in her cupboard, has she?' he grated under his breath when they had said their goodbyes to Stella and were heading for a taxi rank at the end of the boulevard.

For a second Fran was shocked, but only a second. Drawing a deep breath she said, 'Jean-Claude, you mean? You're implying there was something between us?' Her expression was disdainful. 'We were friends at school and that was all. And *you* can talk about skeletons. You and Stella seemed pretty close, all that kissing and bonhomie.' She didn't throw Helena in his face; that would be too painful.

To her chagrin he laughed softly. 'That bothered you, did it?' he asked rhetorically. 'You know, I thought you were such a tough, streetwise little wretch when I first met you—was it only hours ago? But you're just a sweet old-fashioned girl at heart, aren't you? Do you cuddle down at night in your Victorian lace nightie and dream of orange blossom and white weddings?'

Fran was speechless. She couldn't understand why he was suddenly mocking her and so bitterly too.

'No, I don't,' she whispered at last. 'And would there be so very much wrong with it if I did?'

'Nothing at all.' He shrugged dismissively but the muscles in his face tightened as he said it.

They reached the taxi rank in silence and Fran collapsed into the back of a taxi. She had never felt so tired in all her life. It had been a long day, a confusing night that had somehow soured at the gallery. It was as if her whole life had somersaulted on a pin-head. She closed her eyes, not wanting to think about that awful Stella making a play for Jordan right under her nose, and somewhere in the bottomless pit of her confused thoughts was her sister as well.

She was warm and cosy, wrapped in his arms. Lips were on hers, soft and sensuous, a hand gently caressed her throat. The sensations were deliciously dream-like and she didn't want them to stop. The kiss grew deeper, more urgent and she responded, manoeuvring her arms to clasp him tighter, parting her lips to taste the sweetness and the ecstasy.

Slowly, oh, so slowly, consciousness nudged at her and the warmth began to slip away. She grasped at it, once again feeling that divine pressure on her mouth. The hand moved from the silkiness of her throat to the front of her dress, softly, rhythmically smoothing the rise and fall of her breasts beneath. Unwillingly she blinked open her eyes and harsh reality smacked her in the face. She was awake... in the back of the taxi... in Jordan Parry's arms!

She tried to struggle away but he held her firmly. 'Take it easy,' he whispered.

'Take it easy! How—how dare you do that?' she shrieked. 'I—I was asleep... Why... why, you're a—a necro—a necromantic!'

'I think you mean a necrophiliac, Miss Kinky Mind, and you're not dead, you were merely dozing and well aware of what was going on,' he ground out, trying to control her flaying arms.

'You're the kinky one,' Fran cried in exasperation as he held her strongly. 'I meant what I said, a necromantic, a damned sorcerer! Now unhand me and let me out of this cab!'

With incredible strength she managed to push him to the corner of the seat as the taxi pulled into the kerb outside the Clermont. Wrenching open the door, she accidentally ground the heel of her shoe into his foot as she lurched on to the pavement.

He groaned in agony, clutching at his foot.

'And don't play for sympathy!' she hissed. 'I won't fall into your arms so easily again. Helena might be a pushover, but I'm not! You're too damned right I dream of orange blossom!'

With that she swept majestically up the steps of the Hotel Clermont and through the revolving doors, missing *his* parting shot, called out in the cold Paris night air.

'Well, marry me, then!'

CHAPTER FOUR

JORDAN dabbed at his jawline with a towel and rinsed out his razor in the sink. He glared at himself in the bathroom mirror, seeing a fool.

'You've got to be out of your mind,' he growled. He closed his eyes to blot out thoughts of the previous night. He'd proposed to a slip of a girl he barely knew. Thank God she hadn't heard—he had enough on his mind already. When he opened his eyes again, all was clear: she would have to go.

'Morning, Silas.' He greeted his assistant with a perfunctory smile as he strode into the lounge of the suite.

Silas glanced up from the desk where he was sorting through paperwork and nodded towards coffee set out on the low glass table.

'Good morning, Jordan,' he returned. 'How are you feeling—nervous?'

Jordan poured himself a coffee and took it to the window. He drank it hot, black and unsweetened while looking down at the boulevard below, almost the same view as from her room.

'Nervous?' he repeated after a long pause. 'What's nervous?'

Silas regarded him curiously, shrugged and went on with his work. 'The disks are perfect, incidentally; the paperwork too. I went through them last night while you were out. Helena did well after the computer room mess-up. Stroke of genius sending her sister over with them. If they had got lost...' He didn't continue for they both knew the implication of that. 'What's she like?'

'Who?' Jordan asked absently.

'The sister. As good-looking as Helena?'

Jordan was tempted to tell him to wrap up. How could you compare the two? One a hard, glossy magazine-cover beauty, the other with all the warmth, freshness and sweet loveliness of a morning primrose... Hell! He slammed his coffee-cup down on the table. She would definitely have to go!

"I'm looking forward to meeting her,' Silas remarked with a smile.

'You won't get the chance,' Jordan snapped. 'She's leaving today.'

Silas, taken aback, said, 'But last night you said she had agreed to stay on for the conference. What changed her mind?'

'I changed *my* mind. She's unsuitable, only a kid,' he clipped.

Silas let the matter drop for there were more pressing things to attend to. He pushed a sheaf of papers across the desk as Jordan approached.

'Peter Brabben booked in last night and will attend the conference,' he told Jordan, and for the first time that morning the head of Parry Pharmaceuticals looked pleased.

'Arrange some personal meetings with him, Silas. He's the one.'

Brabben was the financial director of Unimet, one of the largest group of holding companies in the world and the one most likely to meet Jordan's terms. There were the employees to consider, the hospice for sick children his father had built and subsidised all these years; Jordan didn't want them to lose out in the take-over, and they wouldn't if all went well with the new drug and Unimet were interested enough to talk. But first there was a wretch to be rid of!

Fran awoke to insistent rapping at the door. For a few seconds she was unsure of her whereabouts and then it came flooding back to her—everything!

She took her time climbing out of bed. Breakfast already—it felt like the middle of the night. She peered at her watch on the bedside table. Seven o'clock. It *was* the middle of the night!

'*Un moment, s'il vous plaît,*' she called out as the rapping became more impatient. She padded across the room prepared to tell room service they had made a mistake, she'd ordered breakfast for nine not seven.

'Oh, it's you.' She yawned, wishing she'd brought a dressing-gown with her—the flimsy, primrose-yellow nightie she was wearing left little to the imagination. 'What are you staring at?' she asked crisply. 'Or is that a silly question?'

'Cover yourself up,' Jordan ordered as he stepped into her bedroom. 'I might have been a waiter.'

She couldn't see the logic of that. He was bad enough. Nevertheless she pulled a sweater over the top of the thin cotton. It looked silly but she didn't care, she wasn't trying to impress him. It looked sillier still in comparison with what he was wearing: an impeccable pearl-grey suit, fresh white shirt and a marine-blue silk tie.

'Have you come to apologise for your behaviour last night in the back of the taxi?' she asked him openly. No point in beating about the bush, no other reason heralded such an early morning call. Well, she had her answer ready. Boys will be boys, she would say.

'Apologise for giving you what you were screaming out for?' he said coldly.

Fran had a choice, to ignore that or slap the insult from his face. Then she saw the bulky brown envelope he was holding in one hand and her angry blood cooled.

'What's that?' she asked, a fearful dread running through her because she had a good idea what it was.

He tossed it on the crumpled bed dismissively. 'It's your freedom,' he said.

Fran's wide green eyes flickered uncertainly from his expressionless features to the envelope and back again. 'My freedom? I don't understand.'

'It's your passport and your money. You can get the first flight home this morning.'

The need to sit down was overwhelming but Fran's legs wouldn't budge her. She stood motionless and looked at him bleakly. He wanted her to leave and the pain of that knowledge made her feel sick.

'But last night you were adamant. You wanted me to stay and help. Why the sudden change of heart?' she pleaded to know, eyes innocent and misty.

Jordan turned away, unable to stand the look in her lovely eyes. The only place to go was the window, but she caught him before he reached it.

'Why, Jordan?' she husked, tugging at his sleeve, forcing him to face her.

He took a jagged breath, couldn't meet her eyes. 'Because you're not up to the job. You're just not suitable. You were right in the first place,' he gritted his teeth, 'you'd make a fool of yourself and me. You're a risk I can do without at the moment.' He went to move towards the door but Fran wasn't about to let him get away with that. She barred his way with her body, heard his sharp intake of breath.

'No, you don't!' she burst out. 'I didn't make a fool of myself in the restaurant, did I? I know I can be a bit outspoken at times but I do know when to curb it. I work in one of the most prestigious galleries in South Ken. I wouldn't be able to hold down a job like that if I wasn't good with clients . . . and the wine bar—you have to be on your toes——' Suddenly she stopped in mid-sentence, her heart skittering wildly. Why on earth was she hyping herself up for him when this was exactly what she wanted, wasn't it? Her passport home!

The awful truth dawned and she leapt away from him as if she had been stung. She didn't want to go. She wanted to stay, here in Paris, with him. She turned her back on him, faced the wall like a naughty child, curled her arms around herself to deaden the pain inside her.

'You'd better get out of my room and quick before I really lose my temper,' she threatened with as much menace as she could bring to her voice, which was little because his dismissal had been like a blow to the kidneys—she could scarcely breathe.

It was a long time before he spoke, a long time in which Fran wrestled hopelessly with her new-found feelings.

'I've put some extra cash in the envelope. A small payment . . .'

She swung on him viciously, her breath back in a rush. 'The back of the taxi?' Her eyes narrowed painfully. 'You...you stinker.' She gave out a small hysterical sob. 'I see it all now—why you want me to go. It would be different if I'd slept with you last night, wouldn't it?'

'Fran!' he bellowed warningly.

'Don't Fran me! You wouldn't be half as anxious to be rid of me if——'

He was on top of her before she knew it, his hands gripping her so roughly by the shoulders, it was pure self-control on his part that he didn't shake the life from her like a dog with a rabbit.

'You have an abominable mind for such an innocent face, Fran Cain. You deserve a thrashing for a remark like that. I don't have to pay for any favours, believe me.'

'No doubt they're handed to you on a plate,' Fran bit back. 'Let me go, you're hurting me!'

'Men have killed for less,' he rasped angrily. 'Now say sorry for your warped accusations.' He squeezed her burning flesh harder and Fran wondered where she had got the impression Jordan Parry was an unemotional, unfeeling cold fish.

'OK, OK, I'm sorry,' she cried quickly.

He let her go with a grunt and a final dismissive push. She stood rubbing her painful shoulders.

'You don't know your own strength,' she muttered ruefully.

'Now who's playing for sympathy.' He picked up the phone and ordered coffee for two.

'I'm not expecting anyone,' she goaded wilfully.

'Shut up, Fran,' he thundered. 'I've had enough lip from you.' He raked a hand through his hair, disrupting its glossy smoothness in a gesture of exasperation. 'I'm sorry if I hurt you just now and I'm more than sorry for last night. I should never have let it happen. It's not often I lose my senses.'

All Fran's anger and strength went then. Huge tears welled at the back of her eyes but bravely she stemmed them. Time enough for tears when she reached London. How stupid and naïve she had been, allowing herself to fall for this man. He didn't care for her, not one bit.

She took up the envelope from the bed and up-ended the contents on to the drawn-back sheets. She threw the wad of French francs, separated from her other belongings by a band of paper, across the covers towards him.

'I did this for Helena,' she told him softly. 'I don't expect a payment from you . . .'

'Take it.'

'No!' she cried, then lowered her voice. 'I don't want any reminders. I just want to get out of your life as quickly as you want to see the back of me.'

He took a step towards her. 'Look, Fran, it isn't what you think . . .'

'Don't come near me, Jordan Parry.' She gathered up her passport and her own money and shoved them deep into her shoulder-bag. 'I don't know why you wanted me to stay in the first place. You want me, then you don't. How you run a multimillion pound organisation I can't imagine...' She turned and looked at him, sudden puzzlement clouding her eyes. This was the head of Parry Pharmaceuticals, a man with a brain, a man who had to make crucial decisions every day of his life. A very special sort of man. So why...?

'Jordan,' she said quietly, urged on by a need for the truth, 'why the change of heart? You asked me to stay on and help you and now you're telling me you made a mistake, made a wrong character judgement. I can't believe that and it has nothing to do with what happened in the taxi either, has it?'

There was a long pause before he answered. 'I certainly didn't make a wrong character judgement, did I? You're smart, all right.' He moved to her and took her shoulders again. She flinched, expecting pain. 'It has everything to do with what happened in the back of the taxi,' he said huskily.

'What do you mean?' she uttered weakly, already her senses spinning at his intimate closeness.

He crushed her against him. 'It's all about this,' he grated, grazing his mouth against her ear. 'Are you willing to take it further, Fran?'

She pushed at his chest. 'I don't understand you.'

He looked down at her, his eyes hooded and dark. 'Are you denying this?' His lips brushed hers, so sensually she felt the need rise dangerously. He parted her lips softly, explored the moist softness of the inside of her mouth, held her hard against him till she trembled uncontrollably in his arms. She felt the mattress pressed into the back of her legs and the thought of the bed so close sent a shiver of desire through her.

His hands moved under her sweater and his kisses deepened to a hunger that made her head spin. The fragile panel of lace at the front of her nightie tore under pressure and his hand slid over her breast and her hardened nipple—confidently.

She wrenched her mouth from his and bit back tears of pain and misery. 'Why are you doing this, Jordan?' she bleated. Was it some sort of punishment?

'I'm proving a point, Fran,' he rasped thickly. 'If you stay here in Paris I'm going to have to make love to you. I don't play games either. All or nothing.' His mouth came across hers again, arousing her so swiftly and painfully she thought she would pass out with the deep ache of longing inside her. She clung to him, half in fear, half in madness. How easily Helena must have succumbed to him. Oh, God—Helena.

'You bastard!' she breathed against his cheek, trying to wriggle out of his arms. 'Are you trying to say by dismissing me you are protecting my virtue? Since when have you become so pious?

You're having an affair with my sister—she has self-respect too, but you don't think of her.'

'Having an affair with your sister!' he echoed incredulously, his grip on her arms slackening. 'Is that what you meant in the taxi, a pushover like your sister?'

Fran didn't answer; she bit her lip, wishing with all her heart she'd never brought Helena into this.

Jordan glared at her, fury gathering in the storm-grey of his eyes. He let her go, stemmed his anger, his mouth hardening to a thin line of coldness. 'Your sister has nothing to do with us. If you stay on in Paris, you know what to expect from me...'

'In other words, part of the job is sleeping with you?' Fran grazed back painfully. How could he coldly suggest such a thing? 'I couldn't do that,' she told him, shaking her head. 'I want to stay and help but not this way, not on those terms.'

His cold grey eyes ranged over her face. 'Last night you didn't want to stay, you said you had a million reasons why you couldn't. You talk of me changing my mind, but what wind changed yours? It wouldn't have anything to do with discovering a past lover is here in Paris and accessible, would it?' he bit out icily.

She slapped him then, hard across the face, and he didn't even flinch. 'He was not my lover and he has nothing at all to do with my change of heart,' Fran seethed. 'I changed my mind because of something you wouldn't understand in a thousand years. You're too busy tying up company mergers, balancing the books, playing corporate games. People are to be *used* in your suffocating little life, aren't they?' Her eyes glittered wildly and then she looked away quickly. She'd given too much away, her feelings were lying dangerously close to her lips. Jean-Claude had been light years away from her decision to stay. He, Jordan Parry, was the only reason she wanted to be here, but he didn't want her; as a plaything for a few days, but that was all.

A knock at the door smashed the hostility between them and Fran was the first to move. She opened the door to the waiter with their coffee. While he placed the tray on the small table by the window, Jordan straightened his tie. He tipped the waiter and waited till he'd left the room before speaking.

'The choice is yours whether to stay or go,' he said in a voice that gave nothing away but his bleak resignation. 'I do need your help after the conference but I'm damned sure I'm not financing your reunion with an untalented artist. Any expenses incurred in that region will have to come out of your own pocket.' He crossed to the door, opened it with a jerk, stopped when she called his name.

She asked huskily, tentatively, 'Do you *want* me to stay?'

His knuckles whitened round the edge of the door and Fran's heart slowed, waiting for an

answer that he seemed to find difficult to give.
'Yes, I want you to stay,' he eventually capitu-
lated, but if Fran thought it was personal she was
sadly wrong. 'The company has a trying time
ahead of it. I need all the help I can get.' With
that he closed the door after him.

Shaking with shock at his coldness, Fran had
little chance to settle her spinning senses before
the phone rang.

'Oh, Helena!' she croaked in surprise. 'Are you
calling from the hospital?' Her own voice
sounded unnatural and worse—guilty! Suddenly
the last twenty-four hours crowded in on her, the
full implication of what had happened between
her and her sister's lover hit her. She viciously
smoothed down her sweater as if Helena could
see her.

'Bad news, I'm afraid. I've broken a small
bone in my left foot. I have to have a cast put
on it this morning. Awful nuisance,' she huffed.
'I won't be able to pick you up from the airport.'

'Don't worry, Helena. Get yourself fit and
well. I can——' She was about to add she could
get a taxi but as usual Helena wasn't that interested in anything she did.

'Exactly what Jordan said last night when I
called him,' Helena butted in. 'Poor darling
sounded at the end of his tether. He was terribly
grateful to me for sending you over with the disks.
I said I'd get over as soon as possible, but he said

everything was under control and he'd arranged some temporary help...'

'Yes, me.' Fran made a face down the phone. 'But——' She wanted to tell her she wasn't going to stay but again Helena interrupted, incredulously this time.

'You!' she blurted down the phone, and Fran's spine stiffened as it usually did when Helena used that deprecatory tone with her. 'Jordan asked *you*? You must have made a mistake, dear.'

'Of course I didn't make a mistake. Jordan asked me to stay and help after the lectures——'

'Don't be absurd, Fran. You always were a bit scatty. You obviously misheard...' She rattled on about how only she was capable of assisting Jordan Parry, and had Fran been making a fool and a nuisance of herself? It was at that point that Fran saw red.

'I suppose it has never occurred to you that your sister might have a worth other than looking after an aged parent,' she hit out. 'Jordan asked for my help, believing I was capable of giving it. I speak French, don't forget, which you don't——'

There was what sounded like a muffled explosion at the other end of the line and Fran was delighted to think her only ammunition against Helena, another language, had hit home. And then, as usual, she regretted her outburst almost immediately.

'Helena,' she soothed, 'I couldn't possibly do such a good job as you, even Jordan admits that, but he wants...' Fran gripped the telephone receiver fiercely, unable to go on. Not in a month of Sundays could Helena imagine what had happened between her and Jordan since her arrival in Paris. Helena wasn't apoplectic because she was afraid of losing her lover to her kid sister— that wouldn't occur to her—she was just afraid Fran would make a fool of herself and somehow it might reflect on her. Her assumptions were spot-on.

'Fran, this is not a good idea!' Helena screeched, her panic-level rising hysterically. 'Jordan is a perfectionist. If you step out of line with him, say one wrong word, it could cost me my job!'

Step out of line! One wrong word! She'd slapped the man, called him all the names under the sun...

'Fran! Fran! Are you still there?'

'Yes... yes, I'm here.' But certainly not all there, Fran thought reproachfully. What an idiot she was to let the conversation get this far. Helena was convinced she was staying on to assist Jordan and now if she denied it there would be *some* explaining to do.

'Look, I'm going to phone Jordan now——'

'And what are you going to say? That your little sister is a prize idiot and no use to a living soul? Well, go ahead, Helena, it implies he can't make a decision for himself and I'm sure he'll appreciate *that*. You don't need me to put your job at risk—you're quite capable of doing it yourself.'

'Are you going out of your mind?' her sister gasped raggedly.

'Yes, quite possibly.' And Fran put down the receiver.

She sat for a very long time on the edge of the bed, staring at the floor and holding her head in her hands. Why did she say the things she did? Dig herself into situations she couldn't get out of? She should have told Helena she had no intention of staying right from the outset of that silly conversation. Instead her pride and her need to hit back at her sister had twisted everything. Helena now believed she was staying on to work for Jordan, and if she returned to England this afternoon she would want to know the reason why.

'Because your precious boss demanded more than the statutory working hours, Helena dear, and I'm sure you know what I mean.' Fran shuddered at the thought. Much as she wanted to hit back at Helena, she knew how much her sister cared for Jordan. And yet he had neither confirmed nor denied the affair—but what did it matter anyway?

She got up and stood by the window, watched the rush-hour traffic gather momentum on the boulevard below. It mattered. She hugged herself for comfort. It mattered painfully.

She reflected on the row between her and Jordan that morning. If she didn't know the man better she would say he was terrified of a serious commitment to a woman, any woman. But that couldn't be true; a man like him wouldn't be afraid of anything and yet, in a curious way, she felt he was afraid of her. He'd made it clear that he found her attractive—she wasn't that naïve that she believed his kisses meant nothing—but he'd also made it clear that the emotional side of the job was part of the whole package—come the end of the conference, her terms of employment ceased, in all ways.

Fran's heart ached. How easy it would be to accept those conditions, to work with him and to love him as he had requested. But it wouldn't be enough, she knew that with a passion that gave no pleasure. Was it possible to fall in love so quickly, so easily, so agonisingly?

I'm not in love with him, she breathed into the air resolutely. It's a feeling, a need, but it couldn't be love, surely? She wished she knew, wished there was a book you could buy, one that asked a lot of questions and at the end you totalled your score and knew for sure. And what would she do with that knowledge? Would it make any difference how she handled this situation?

To stay or not to stay, that is the question! she misquoted in her fevered mind. She bit her lip fiercely, tried to think positively. Make a list, a list of pros and cons.

Taking her sketch-pad out and a pen, she made two lists. The pros were easy: Paris in the spring, accommodation in the elegant Clermont, time to sketch and indulge herself in the art galleries. The cons were easy too, only one: Jordan Parry!

It was all up to her, really. She sighed and ripped the page from the pad and screwed it into a tight ball. She wanted to stay on in Paris, it was an artist's dream city and what chance had she of affording to come again? It was hard enough saving up to buy her freedom out of Helena's flat. Next year she would have enough for a deposit on a small flat in the suburbs somewhere, no holidays for aeons. But that was hardly reason enough to suffer what she would inevitably have to suffer, seeing Jordan every night and falling deeper and deeper in love with him. Except she might not, she thought hopefully. She might learn to hate him over the next few days.

She got up, went through to run a bath. A long hot soak in fragrant water decided her. She would stay and help him and she would keep a very tight rein on her emotions. He need never know how she felt about him and she would never allow a situation to arise where he might guess. She would be strong—she'd never considered herself a weakling anyway—and she would fight her feelings and, as for his threats to make love to her, well, once again, that was up to her. She had refused, and if another close encounter should occur she would... Her thoughts didn't rationalise any further. Her head was spinning.

She was sitting by the window, sharing her warm croissants with the pigeons on the windowsill, when the phone purred. It was Stella to say she'd meet her in Reception in an hour. After unwillingly agreeing Fran put down the receiver. So deep in her thoughts, Fran had almost forgotten Stella's existence.

It brought Jean-Claude to mind. Jordan hadn't been far from the truth when he had insinuated he was a past lover. Like most of the female fraternity at art school, Fran had had a crush on the fascinating Frenchman. Nothing had come of it. Jean-Claude had treated her like one of the numerous cousins he'd left behind in Lyons, though there had been that time in the bronze sculpture studio when he had tilted her face to the light and murmured that she had the most exquisite bone-structure he had ever seen. His fingers had lingered and caressed and Fran was sure he would have kissed her if it hadn't been for a sudden rush of students filling the studio for a lecture. Soon after, tragedy had struck the Lefarge family and Jean-Claude had left, and like all the other girls she had soon forgotten him.

Raking up the past wasn't one of Fran's preoccupations, but the day yawned interminably ahead of her and she had to admit that Jean-Claude's painting had intrigued her. His work had changed and she was just a little curious, and what harm would it do to go along with Stella and pass a pleasant half-hour with an old schoolfriend?

She dressed quickly in jeans and sweater and brushed out her light golden hair, glanced at her watch and found she had quite a while to kill before meeting Stella.

Gathering up the money Jordan had left behind, she rammed it into her bag. She would return it to him later but for the time being it was safer with her rather than leaving it lying around.

She took the lift down to the basement where the conference facilities were housed. Security at the Clermont was tight and Fran was challenged by a uniformed guard as soon as she stepped out of the lift.

'You have a pass?' the guard asked firmly.

'Oh, no, I haven't. I . . . I work for Parry Pharmaceuticals.' She flushed deeply, wishing she hadn't acted so impulsively. She had wanted to see the start of the conference, Jordan's opening speech, but instead she was about to be embarrassed, asked to leave the premises.

'You have your passport with you?' the guard asked, his face impassive.

Fran plunged her hand into her shoulder-bag. Mercifully she had. The guard studied it, ran a podgy finger down a list. Fran saw to her astonishment her name added to the bottom page. Jordan Parry certainly was efficient, and confident she would stay, too. The guard smiled, handed her back her passport and indicated double doors at the end of the corridor.

'It is full,' he told her. 'But there is room to stand at the back.'

Fran slipped in and her eyes settled on the tall speaker on the rostrum, and for seconds she didn't realise who she was staring at.

He was a stranger, a formidable stranger holding everyone's attention with his compelling speech. His voice production was superbly fluent. The auditorium was packed with eminent men and women, taking notes, watching intently, some clasping their simultaneous translating facilities to their ears for fear of missing a word.

This was the Jordan Parry who had held her in his arms not so very long ago. The Jordan Parry she had slapped and insulted. The Jordan Parry who was so far out of reach he might as well have been on another planet.

She took deep breaths outside in the corridor. Somehow she found her way to the ground floor and Reception, her thoughts and feelings so muzzy she couldn't think straight.

'I really wanted to see Jordan before we left,' a voice said behind her and Fran swung to face Stella. So she hadn't been wrong. Stella's friendly overtures were for the sole purpose of contriving further meetings with Jordan.

'He's lecturing, I'm afraid,' Fran told her.

Stella shrugged her shoulders, not put off in the least. 'Not to worry, I'll catch him when I drop you back later. I've just heard of the most divine set of first edition prints he might be interested in...'

She gabbled on as they went out of the front doors of the Clermont, but Fran hardly registered a word. As they stepped out on to the wide pavement Fran glanced up into the grey skies of Paris and inwardly called herself all the fools under the sun. She should have gone home, not persuaded herself to stay. Now it was too late. She had an endless day ahead of her with Stella and Jean-Claude and she couldn't wriggle out of it—and then there was tonight and Jordan Parry.

As she reluctantly followed Stella to her car she wondered if there was a passing motorcycle courier she could throw herself under!

CHAPTER FIVE

STELLA shot her nippy Renault into gear and pulled out into the traffic without a backward glance. Car horns hooted in their ears but Stella was oblivious.

'So how come you're here in Paris with Jordan?' Stella asked Fran openly.

What she really wanted to know was how deeply she and Jordan were involved. Fran wasn't in a mood for games. She told her about her sister Helena being Jordan's secretary and her accident and the floppy disks.

'Without Helena, Jordan needs someone to help out with the socialising. He asked me to stay on. I'll be going back to my own job when the conference is over,' she concluded.

'So you're not romantically involved with him?'

Fran couldn't help but smile. That told Fran that Stella *wasn't*! 'He's too old for me,' she stated flatly, hoping Stella would be satisfied with that and leave her alone.

'You're right. He's the type to appreciate an older woman.'

You, I suppose, Fran thought, only half listening to Stella's detailed account of her divorce from a French lawyer, the gallery she opened because she loved Paris so and how she had met Jordan two years ago when he had first started buying from her.

Fran was tempted to say that if she hadn't hooked him by now she never would, but she didn't of course. Just nodded and agreed and made predictable comments when they were sought.

It seemed that Stella warmed to her more now that she knew Fran wasn't a threat. Fran wasn't sure how she felt about that.

The grey block of apartments where Jean-Claude lived was set in an unglamorous area on the outskirts of the city centre. It was a tall, narrow building with no lifts and they trudged up the dank concrete stairs, the smell of garlic and boiled cabbage overwhelming. Fran wished she were anywhere but here.

Jean-Claude's apartment was the top one. Stella hammered on the door. There was no answer. Fran was relieved, and she turned away from the shabby, paint-chipped door. 'He's obviously not in, Stella. Your knocking would have woken the dead.'

Fran regretted her choice of words when the door suddenly opened. The Jean-Claude who stood there was a ghost of the handsome Jean-Claude she had adored at college. His tawny hair had darkened to a dull brown, his golden skin had sallowed and the mouth that had laughed so easily was drawn into a tight line.

The hallway was so dark Stella had to announce herself, adding, 'I've brought an old friend of yours with me.'

It was only when Fran stepped into the light from the shadows that a smile of recognition brightened his face.

'Fran! I can hardly believe it! Here in Paris... Let me look at you.' He held her by the shoulders with fingers that held no strength, and though Fran tried to look happy to meet him again she felt concern thread through her. He looked so very different. So much older and duller.

'Do come in.' He stepped back and ushered them in.

'Fran recognised one of your canvases in my gallery,' Stella explained. 'Quite a coincidence, isn't it? Have you finished those pictures I asked you for? I can't promise I'll sell them...'

Jean-Claude took Stella to the far end of the room where several canvases stood against the wall. It was then that Fran recognised the reason for her friend's depressive appearance. The state of the sparsely furnished apartment-cum-studio confirmed her suspicions. He was broke.

Jean-Claude made coffee, talking incessantly, asking Fran how mutual acquaintances were progressing. Stella browsed through the canvases, setting aside several she was interested in.

'I lost touch with everyone when I left to look after my father,' Fran told him, helping with the coffee, noting Jean-Claude's kitchen cupboards were thinly stocked, the mugs they were about to drink from chipped and stained.

'Me, too,' Jean-Claude commiserated, his hazel eyes watery with past thoughts.

'I'm sorry about your brother, Jean-Claude. You left college so quickly I never had a chance to say before. You must miss him very much.'

He put on a look of bravado that Fran recognised as a cover-up. 'Yes, I do,' he admitted. 'But life goes on. I still can't get over seeing you, Fran, still can't get over the coincidence of your recognising one of my pictures in Stella's gallery.'

Fran laughed. 'Yes, quite unbelievable, isn't it?' She looked at him and for a moment she felt that deep ache associated with past memories, the feelings she'd had for him, the good times they'd had together with the old crowd.

'So you're staying at the glorious Clermont,' he said after Fran had filled in some of the details of why she was here in Paris. 'Certainly landed on your feet, didn't you?'

They sat on a hard sofa and drank their coffee. Fran laughed and padded out her previous explanation of why she was in Paris. 'If my sister hadn't had a duel with a motorcycle courier I wouldn't be here now,' she ended.

It was as they chatted on and Jean-Claude seemed to tense more and more that Fran's suspicions were aroused. He had changed so much, too drastically for it to be a simple case of just being a couple of years older. She tried to pinpoint her unease and eventually she came up with a thought that truly disturbed her. It was a thought she didn't want to admit to and one she didn't want to pursue in her mind till later. He was depressed, of that she was sure, and he talked a lot about his dead brother. After all this time he still seemed deeply affected by it.

At last Stella wanted to leave. 'I'll take these three, Jean-Claude, but as I said I can't promise anything.'

'Can't you give me something on account?' Jean-Claude pleaded and Fran's heart wrenched painfully. He was probably in debt, owed rent and was obviously not feeding himself properly. He was so gaunt.

Stella hesitated for a moment. 'You know I don't normally... Sale or return...' She saw the pleading look in Fran's eyes and relented, opened her Gucci bag and delved for some cash.

'I'd like to see you again before you leave Paris,' he whispered to Fran as Stella was sorting out her money.

'Yes... yes, that would be nice,' Fran faltered. She would have liked to have seen the old Jean-Claude again but this one troubled her deeply. He needed help, she was sure, but was she the one to offer it? 'I'll give you the phone number of the Clermont and my room number—you can give me a ring.' She fumbled in her bag for a scrap of paper, spilling the contents of her bag over the sofa in her haste. She scooped it all back again, hoping Jean-Claude hadn't seen that wad of Jordan Parry's money; the sooner that was returned to its owner the better.

Outside in the street after saying their goodbyes, Fran breathed deeply. She turned to Stella. 'Thank you for bringing me to see him.' She let out a deep sigh. 'He's changed,' she murmured.

'Yes, well, that's the way it is these days,' Stella said dismissively and walked towards the car, obviously anxious to get Fran back to the Clermont.

'I won't come back with you, Stella.' Fran followed her to the car. 'I need to do some shopping—a couple of dresses for the evenings.'

Stella laughed. 'You won't find anything round here. Get in and I'll drop you off at Galeries Lafayette, it's en route.'

Yes, en route to the Clermont, Fran guessed, but somehow didn't care. Her thoughts for once weren't on Jordan Parry but her old college friend.

Stella dropped her off outside the department store and sped off without a wave.

Fran bought two dresses: traffic-stopper red and a floaty oyster-coloured affair that soared her bank credit into debit. It felt decadent spending so much money after seeing Jean-Claude in such dire straits, but it was necessary. She couldn't wear her black dress every night.

She took a taxi back to the hotel and picked over the bones of her conversation with Jean-Claude. It was over two years since his brother had died and yet he gave the impression it was only yesterday.

Fran knew all about grief. Hadn't she been through all that when her father had died? Hadn't she hated herself for waking up the next morning with relief flooding through her and hadn't she missed him so terribly, even missed the abuse he'd rained on her when his constant pain had driven him to despair?

She had coped but Jean-Claude hadn't, and wasn't his request to see her again a plea for her help? She decided that if he did get in touch with her she would see him; perhaps she could help him, listen to his problems.

Damn! Fran stood outside her bedroom door and stared into her handbag furiously. She'd lost her room key. It was probably down the back of Jean-Claude's sofa, dropped there when she had spilled the contents of her bag. She cursed herself a hundred times as she took the lift down to Reception to get a spare. Heavens, it was big enough, how could she have been so stupid?

'So you decided to stay,' he said, stepping into the lift behind her.

Fran swung round, and colour sprang to her cheeks as she faced Jordan. He looked drawn and tired and Fran felt a rush of feeling for him. He had been working so hard all day and she had been wasting her time with Stella and Jean-Claude.

'Yes...I...' She couldn't think of a reason to give him why.

'I hear you had a pleasant time with your old friend,' he drawled sarcastically.

'Stella?'

'Yes, Stella,' he said ruefully. 'You might have spared me that. The last thing I want at the moment is a set of first edition prints by some obscure Czechoslovakian itinerant.'

'She fancies you.' Fran laughed and was pleased to see his face crumple into a smile.

'Does she, now? I'm surprised,' he teased. 'And what else have you been up to?' He eyed the carrier in her hand.

'I needed a couple of dresses. Stella dropped me off at a department store.' She felt guilty for her self-indulgence and he probably thought she had spent his money as well. The lift wasn't the place to ram it back at him—she'd do that later.

'I look forward to seeing you in them—or out of them, come to that.'

He was still teasing her, at least she thought he was, or maybe just trying to frighten her away.

His eyes momentarily narrowed. 'And where are you going now?' The lift clunked to a halt on the ground floor and the gates opened.

'I forgot to pick up my key from Reception.' She prayed he wasn't going to the desk too. She didn't want him to know she had been stupid enough to lose her key. 'How did the lecture go, Jordan?' she asked as they walked across the plush carpeting.

'Very well,' he said on a sigh as if he was relieved it was over.

Fran stopped and touched his arm. 'I'm glad,' she said softly.

He held her gaze and said quietly, 'I'm glad you're glad. I'm going out now. I need some fresh air and a change of scenery. See my assistant Silas Matthews when you go upstairs—he's in my suite and will give you all the information on tonight. I'll see you later.' He walked away and Fran watched him go, wishing she could have gone with him, wishing he had asked her.

Fran liked Silas Matthews on sight. He was middle-aged, slightly paunchy, with thinning silver hair and the most wonderful sparkling blue eyes.

'Come in, Fran,' Silas urged when he opened the suite door. 'Yes, I can see the likeness. I've just spoken to Helena on the phone. Now what is all this confusion about whether or not you are staying? Jordan seemed to think you weren't this morning.'

'Well, we had a little disagreement and——'

'Oh, I'm not surprised.' Silas chuckled. 'Jordan is hardly the most agreeable of employers at the moment. So much on his mind that I wonder how he copes, but cope he does even if he does tear everyone's head off in the process. Still, you're here and that's all that matters. Can I get you a drink?'

Fran sank gratefully on to the sofa and said she'd love some juice if there was any. Suddenly she was very thirsty and tired. With any luck she would have time for a rest before the evening started.

She found Silas so easy to talk to that she began to relax and unwind, and by the time she finished her juice and had listened to his light-hearted instructions for the cocktail party she was almost looking forward to it. It was as she expected, she thought, smiling to herself as she went back to her room: Silas and Jordan would take care of any sales talk and Fran was expected to make sure everyone was happy. A glorified waitress!

Fran unpacked the two dresses she had bought and hung them up in the wardrobe. She'd wear the red tonight, she decided. It was clingy and brushed her knees and was sleeveless with a high neck. She'd wear her hair up to add sophistication to the dress's simplicity. Satisfied with her choice, she flopped on the bed and closed her eyes and forced everything from her mind. It wasn't easy.

She slept and that pleased her, but she awoke feeling crumpled. After showering she applied her make-up with more care than usual and spent time coiling her golden hair and clipping it high on her head with a gilt clasp.

It was only when she was ready and smoothing down the silky textured dress that panic seized her. How could she ever have imagined she could do it? Silas had said there was a sprinkling of sirs coming tonight. Did one curtsy to a sir? She pulled a face at herself in the mirror. Idiot! She'd sold a painting to an earl last week. An earl in a shabby tweed jacket with the elbows out. They were all human under their titles—a thought that would help her through the evening.

She was ready and taking a last look at herself when she realised the shoulder-bag was all wrong and it was the only one she had. She took out her room key and tucked her bag into the bedside cupboard.

'And don't lose this one,' she murmured to herself as she went down the corridor, swinging the key on her finger.

'You look delightful,' Jordan told her when she got to the suite. But the compliment didn't please her—it could have been honeyed with a smile. But then she realised he was on edge and mentally forgave him.

Catering staff were busying themselves around the suite and Fran was grateful for their presence. Jordan seemed preoccupied with his thoughts.

She felt suddenly awkward with him. It unnerved her and her spirits sank lower and lower as she stood by the window waiting for the first guests to arrive. He really had meant her to go this morning. She should have done. She was going to be an embarrassment to him just as he had said.

It all changed when the guests started to arrive. Jordan's tension eased and his attitude towards her softened. If she didn't know better she would have thought he was quite proud to introduce her to his guests. But it was all an act, she reminded herself, she was simply part of the Parry package.

She didn't let him down, Fran was sure of that. She circulated and did what was expected of her. She certainly wasn't expected to hand round the canapés. The caterers did that, a small army of efficiency that moved round the room unobtrusively. No expense had been spared. The light buffet at the end of the suite was exquisitely prepared and displayed and no doubt tasted divine; Fran didn't know, for she was far too nervous to eat. She didn't drink either, only a mineral water laced with nothing stronger than an ice-cube and a sliver of lemon.

It was remarkable how Fran's two jobs in England held her in good stead. Talking art and wine in Paris, you couldn't go wrong, she chuckled to herself, beginning to enjoy the evening.

'How's it going?' Silas whispered in her ear when for one brief moment she was free of male company.

'No problem.' She grinned happily. At that moment she caught Jordan's eye across the room. He raised his glass to her and it was the first genuine gesture of approval of her all evening. She smiled back and unable to hold the gaze lowered her lashes shyly.

Silas moved away to rescue a Scottish doctor's wife, who looked as if she was struggling, conversation-wise, with a Teutonic mountain.

Fran wasn't alone for more than a second. She was joined by Sir Hugh, who she'd been introduced to earlier, and his tiny birdlike wife, Lady Cynthia. Flavio de Boisvert, a consultant from Lyons, stood with them and Fran was soon translating from French to English and vice-versa.

Before she knew it the crowds had thinned and the evening was nearly over. Fran's brain was bursting with the strain of switching languages so often, and her calves ached. She slumped down on to the sofa and Silas poured her her first glass of champagne.

'Oh, Silas, I need this.' Satisfied that the last guest had left, she kicked off her shoes with relief.

Silas laughed. 'Helena would never have done that. She would have suffered to the bitter end.'

'More fool her.' Fran laughed. 'One of life's pure pleasures.' She wriggled her toes ecstatically. 'It sounds as if you know my sister pretty well.'

'Sadly, not well enough,' Silas stated conspiratorially. He poured himself a brandy and joined her. The catering staff moved quietly around the suite clearing up. There was no sign of Jordan. 'A very elusive lady is your sister. I've offered her diamonds, fast cars, vacations in far-off exotic lands——'

Fran threw her head back and laughed. 'Stop teasing, Silas.'

'Who's teasing, little one?' Suddenly the twinkle had gone from his eyes. 'She carries the proverbial torch for Jordan, not me.' He looked depressed about that.

Fran didn't know what to say. 'I'm sorry,' she murmured.

'Sorry for me, or sorry for Helena?' Silas challenged, the twinkle creeping back into his eyes.

Smiling across at him, Fran said quietly, 'Given the choice, you and Jordan are equally fascinating.'

It was his turn to throw his head back and laugh. 'Me? Fascinating? I like you, little Fran Cain. You know, you should do PR work. There are many openings for young ladies of your tact and calibre.'

'I'm happy doing what I'm doing,' she said smiling. Suddenly she wanted to be alone with her suffering. Did the whole world know how much Helena cared for Jordan? She envied her sister, being with him every day of her working life. Fran's love would have to come to an end in a few short days' time. Like Silas, she would have to come to terms with unfulfilled feelings. She stifled a yawn before it gathered momentum. 'Where's Jordan?'

Disappointment rocked her when Silas told her he had gone down to the conference suite to make sure everything was set up for the following day's series of lectures. She felt abandoned, as if she had served her purpose this evening and her company was no longer needed. Which was exactly what had happened, she bleakly told herself.

Suddenly the champagne soured in her mouth. 'I'd better go,' she told Silas quietly and forced her throbbing feet back into her shoes.

'Aren't you going to wait for Jordan?' Silas asked, glancing at his watch.

No doubt Helena would have done, Fran thought bitterly, and have been welcome too.

'No, my job is done. I'm quite exhausted. I want to sleep forever. I'll see you tomorrow.' She forced a smile for Silas.

He struggled to his feet. 'I'll walk you to your room, it's a few doors along from mine.'

'I'm all right, Silas,' she insisted. 'Relax and finish your brandy.' Impulsively she planted a kiss on the side of his face. 'That's for being so nice,' she murmured.

She closed the door of the suite quietly behind her, and looked up to see Jordan coming down the corridor. He looked worn ragged, his tie askew, his evening jacket unbuttoned. His face brightened when he saw her and Fran's pulses raced.

He took her hands in his outside her bedroom door and Fran was so weary she slumped back against the flocked wallpaper.

'You look how I feel.' He smiled.

'That bad?' she said, grinning. 'How do you think it went, good?'

'Very, and all down to you. Thank you for staying. You made it all bearable.' He said it so genuinely that Fran's heart fluttered with pride. He took her in his arms and Fran didn't resist—how could she, feeling the way she did about him? Even the thought of Helena couldn't have prevented her slipping her arms around his neck and melding against him.

His lips were warm and tender on hers and when he finally released her it drained the last ounce of strength from her.

'Time for bed,' he murmured. 'I'll see you tomorrow.' He took her key from her tightly clenched fist and unlocked her bedroom door for her.

'Goodnight, Jordan,' she said softly.

She closed the door behind her, and leaning back against it she closed her eyes and breathed deeply. She loved him for that, his tenderness, his concern, his respect.

'Heavy evening?' The bedside lamp blazed into light and a small cry flew from Fran's lips.

'Jean-Claude! Wh-what are you doing here?' Her heart pounded fear against her rib-cage.

'Only returning your key. You left it on the sofa.' He'd been lying in the darkened room and now he slowly moved to a sitting position on Fran's bed.

Not knowing why, Fran's initial shock and fear at finding him in her room didn't pass. Her heart still thudded and icicles played at the base of her spine.

'You...you could have left it at Reception,' she said weakly. He could have phoned to say he had found it, he could have done any number of things, but he hadn't. He was here and she didn't want him to be.

She licked her lips nervously as she kicked her shoes off once again. She shouldn't be afraid, she thought guiltily, but he had frightened her, lying on her bed just waiting for her.

'We couldn't talk this afternoon with Stella around. I thought I'd return the key and see you again.' He was sitting on the edge of the bed, smiling at her, that old boyish smile she had been familiar with in the past. The anxiety she had noted earlier in his face was gone. He was more like his old self.

Fran smiled back and let the tension drain from her, leaving her body limp. She had been foolish to be afraid of him.

'Would you like some coffee?' She picked up the phone when he nodded and ordered coffee for two. It was the last thing she wanted at this time of night, but strangely she knew she would feel even more relaxed if she knew one of the staff was coming to her room.

'Thank you for coming to see me, Fran,' he said quietly. He leaned his elbows on his knees and stared down at the carpet.

'Oh, Jean-Claude.' Fran sat down beside him, impulsively taking one of his hands in hers. All doubts and fears were gone now. 'You're going through a really bad time, aren't you?'

He gave a wry laugh. 'Understatement of the year.'

'But Jean-Claude, you had so much going for you at college. You were one of the brightest, most talented students,' she reasoned. 'What went wrong? I hate to have to say it, but your work isn't what it used to be.'

He turned to her, and smiled again. 'You always were pretty bright yourself, Fran.' He shook his head slowly. 'Everything went to pieces when I came back to France. I miss Piers. His death broke my mother's heart. My father buried himself in his work. I came to Paris hoping to get some sort of commercial art work, but it was hopeless.'

'Why didn't you come back to college in England?'

'I couldn't afford to. My father was paying my way before, but after Piers died he wasn't interested.'

'But how are you living? Do you manage to make money from your paintings?' Fran asked anxiously, searching her mind for ways to help him.

'It's not so bad in the summer. There are tourists wanting to buy. In the winter I work a few cafés, washing up in the kitchens, sometimes a bit of waiting at tables.'

Fran was appalled. He had had such high hopes; now he was nothing but a wreck, slaving in kitchens.

The coffee arrived and Fran poured two cups and handed one to Jean-Claude. He took it with fingers that trembled. She noticed his nails were bitten almost raw.

'Oh, Jean-Claude, I wish there was something I could do. Perhaps if Stella sells your work you might get known. She has some wealthy clients,' Fran told him optimistically.

'You aren't doing too badly yourself.' He nodded at the surroundings and Fran noted the bitterness in his voice, the shadow that dulled his eyes. His eyes... She stared at them quizzically. He was certainly less agitated than earlier but his eyes were different, the pupils darkly dilated. Fran was now convinced he was taking some sort of drugs. This morning she had been repulsed and hadn't wanted to accept her suspicions, but now she felt a deep pity well inside her.

'I explained to you before, I'm only here by chance. This isn't the way I live, Jean-Claude, this is my sister's life, not mine.'

'Yes, well.' He got to his feet suddenly, raked his thin fingers jerkily through his hair. 'I'd better go. You've got better things to do than to listen to my hard-luck story. Perhaps we'll run into each other again some time...'

'Jean-Claude!' Fran protested, standing up and reaching out to touch the sleeve of his shabby denim jacket. 'Look, don't sound so dismissive, I want to help if I can. I'd like to see you before I go—perhaps we can have lunch together.'

'I don't think so... I have a lot of work on...' His eyes flickered uncertainly. 'Maybe... maybe...' Suddenly his bony shoulders sagged. 'Yes, I'd like that,' he admitted wearily. He pushed his hand into his pocket and came out with a stub of a pencil and piece of paper. He wrote the name and address of a café in Montmartre. 'Thursday, I'll be there Thursday night about eight.' Suddenly he grasped Fran's hands. 'Thanks for being such a good friend, Fran. We'll talk more at the café.'

A protest formed on Fran's lips. Evenings were out, but she hadn't a chance to say before Jean-Claude was at the door. Her mind whirled; could she make an excuse to Jordan and get out of that evening's cocktail party or whatever? Jean-Claude needed her so much.

Fran held open the door for him and he paused in the corridor, then his eyes met hers, and such a desperate plea clouded them that Fran felt her heart lurch. Impulsively she smoothed his cheek with her hand. He grasped her hand and for a second closed his eyes as if he was so grateful she was back in his life. Fran leaned up and kissed him lightly on the cheek, her throat choked with emotion. He smiled at her and walked away. Fran closed the door softly behind him, tears stinging her eyes.

Seconds later the door exploded open and Fran swung round, expecting Jean-Claude, her heart tipping wildly at the sight of a furious Jordan Parry.

'Very touching!' he grated, kicking the door shut behind him. 'I would never have known if I hadn't come out of the suite at that moment. What do I see but a lout leaving your room? The artist?' he stung at her. 'And what's this?' His hand came up and smeared a tear from her cheek. 'Parting is such sweet sorrow,' he rasped so sarcastically that Fran nearly let another fall.

'It's not what you think,' she husked, sweeping her fingers across her eyes.

His eyes flicked to the coffee-cups, the indentation on the bed where Jean-Claude had lain in wait for her. 'Hell, you could hardly wait to get away from me tonight, could you? And you had the audacity to bring him to your room——'

'I didn't bring him here. He brought my key back...' She bit her lip.

Jordan grasped her arm tightly. 'What key, what are you talking about?'

'I left my key behind at his studio——'

'So he could let himself in while you were——'

'No!' Fran protested, eyes wide. She wrenched free of him. 'I didn't give him my key, I lost it. I had no idea he was going to come here. I didn't ask him...'

Jordan's eyes blazed murderously. 'I told you I wasn't financing your renewed romance with the artist and I meant it. Don't you ever see him again, do you understand? If you leave this hotel for one unauthorised minute to see him I'll tear you both limb from limb.' He strode furiously to the door.

'So I'm a prisoner here, am I?' she called out defiantly.

He turned slowly. 'No, Fran.' He was calmer now. 'You are free to do anything you please, anything except meet that shabby lout. Do I make myself clear?'

Fran stared at him in confusion. She had to make him understand. 'He's an old friend, Jordan,' she reminded him. 'Not a lover. I'm telling the truth. I didn't ask him here tonight.'

He didn't believe her. His anger had gone, he looked even more exhausted than earlier, but his eyes still held contempt for her. Fran was so hurt she wanted to cry.

'I saw what I saw, Fran—you in his arms.'

She shook her head. 'I kissed him goodnight, that was all. I felt...'

'Felt what?' He came and stood before her.

Fran bit her lip. She couldn't tell Jordan the truth, that she thought Jean-Claude needed help and she felt sorry for him. It would pose all manner of questions she didn't want to answer. Drugs. How ironic. Poor Jean-Claude probably addicted to them and this man, glowering in front of her, making a living out of manufacturing them.

'I felt nothing, it was merely a gesture,' she breathed at last.

'As it was for me earlier?' he rasped, seizing her before she protested.

His mouth was hot but the feeling behind it coldly punishing. He held her tightly so she couldn't struggle. The long day surged up inside her and tears sprang to her eyes. She wanted it all to be so different—for there to be no Jean-Claude, no Helena, just her and this man.

His mouth suddenly softened in submission as if he didn't hate her any more. And Fran clung to him, letting herself swim in a pool of languid ecstasy as he parted her now willing lips. His hands smoothed her back, loosened the clasp from her hair, letting it fall like a silk curtain around his hands. He held her hair to his lips then traced kisses back to her mouth.

She felt the zip of her dress slacken, a cool breeze catch her bare flesh, and she didn't protest. How could she when every nerve in her body cried yes? He pulled the dress away from her, lowered his head and brushed his lips across the satin-smooth skin of her naked breasts. Fran had never felt anything more exquisite in her life, his tongue sliding over her, his lips drawing her aching nipples. When his mouth came back to hers her lips were parted and expectant.

Slowly he raised her dress back over her shoulders. She felt the cool breeze on her back recede, the zip gently close. She bit her lip in shame for wanting him so very much. She drew back and looked into his eyes, hers wide, mystified and hurt.

He cupped her small face between his two hands, kissed her mouth, her nose, her eyes. 'It wouldn't be right,' he said raggedly. 'I want us to come together unencumbered, not like this, hurt and angry with each other.'

Fran leant her head against the silk of his shirt. Was she expected to admire his sense of honour when she obviously had none? She had wanted him, would have allowed him to want her, regardless of anyone else.

'Yes, of course,' she murmured and moved away from him.

She heard the door close softly behind her but she didn't move straight away. She didn't want to break the spell of feeling his lips still burning hers, but she must—for everyone's sake, she knew she must.

Slowly she undressed and crawled into bed and lay like a stone for the next eight hours.

CHAPTER SIX

FRAN burst into tears when she found out the next morning. It was shortly after she woke up and reached for her watch to see what time it was. She hadn't worn it the night before—it had been too bulky for her outfit—now it was gone. She checked her bag in the bedside cupboard and realised with a dreadful wrench of her heart that everything of value had gone. The watch, a small rolled gold bracelet—a present from her father—all of Jordan Parry's money, her own, even her Metro *carnet* had gone.

Fran sat up in bed, thought of the hotel staff who had access to her room and dismissed them at once. A deep shudder ran through her. Jean-Claude. He had seen Jordan's money in her bag at his studio, and like a fool she had handed the opportunity for him to steal from her on a plate: her hotel key. She'd never had reason to mistrust him at college but he wasn't the Jean-Claude of college any more. He was a friend who had turned to drugs in his time of need.

No wonder he had been so strange the night before. He probably hadn't been waiting for her at all but had heard her coming down the corridor and made out he was returning her key and

wanting to see her again. And at first he had been
unwilling to meet her again when she had
suggested it; he knew he would be under suspicion when she found her valuables gone, and
yet . . .

Fran wiped the last tear from her eyes. And
yet he had seemed pleased when she had insisted,
looked as if he really did need a friend to talk
to.

She gazed at the address of the café he had
given her. Would he be there? But why bother
giving it to her if he didn't mean to meet her?
She knew where he lived, she could always find
him there. No, she had a feeling he would turn
up, that he really was in trouble and needed her.

She would have to tell Jordan. She threw back
the bedcovers and changed her mind before her
feet touched the ground. How could she tell him?
He had enough on his mind without her grizzling
that the shabby lout he had forbidden her to see
had stolen all her worldly goods! And he would
call the police and she didn't want to expose him
to such a scandal when he was in the middle of
the most important conference of his business
life. No, she could say nothing of this to anyone.

The day passed agonisingly slowly. Even a
lunch that Jordan had wished her to attend with
him, a buffet arranged by another drug company
and held in the basement conference centre,
couldn't take her mind off Jean-Claude and make
the day go quicker.

That evening she did her best with her appearance again and yet hardly heard the compliment from Jordan as they stepped into the limousine. He seemed to have forgotten last night but Fran couldn't.

'I like you in that soft pale colour, it makes you look very vulnerable and innocent,' he had whispered out of earshot of Silas, who was going with them to a restaurant as guests of a German research institute.

'I am,' she murmured, settling into the back seat with him. Silas sat up front with David the chauffeur.

'Fran, I'm sorry about last night. I've no claim on you——' He stopped as Fran drew a weary hand across her forehead. 'Is all this getting too much for you? You are looking very pale.' His voice had such a note of deep concern that it brought Fran to her senses with a jolt. His saying he had no claim on her had hurt, but she was being selfish in thinking of herself and Jean-Claude at a time like this. Jordan Parry was the one she should be concerned for. *He* hadn't stolen her things, resorted to drugs when his world had tilted. She managed a bright smile.

'I'm fine,' she assured him. 'In fact I'll go as far as to say I'm really enjoying myself. I thought these cocktail parties and medical get-togethers would be way over my head, but everyone has been so nice.'

Silas let out a deep-throated chuckle from up front. 'Jordan, I think Fran should be put on the permanent staff,' he said without turning his head. '*She* has a wonderful knack of putting people at their ease. I saw Gustav Troyberg actually smile at lunchtime.'

They all laughed because Silas had earlier warned her that the melancholic biochemist from Hamburg was notorious for his sombre attitude. While in conversation with Fran—she couldn't even recall the subject now—his mask had slipped and a man with a dry wit had emerged. Everyone had been pleasantly surprised.

'Seriously though, Fran,' Jordan continued, 'if it's getting too much for you just say the word and take a break.'

'Don't worry,' she smiled, 'I'm fine, honestly.' She bit her lip in the darkness. She had missed a golden opportunity there. She could have feigned exhaustion and squirmed out of the following night's revelry to meet Jean-Claude. But she felt torn between two loyalties: her concern for her old friend and her duty to Jordan. Jordan didn't help her inward struggle by being so nice to her. At lunchtime he had hardly left her side, and Silas had light-heartedly commented on the fact, to which Jordan had replied,

'If you had the choice between Fran and the pomp and ceremony gathered here today which way would you lean, Silas?'

Silas had grinned, given Fran's wrist a gentle squeeze and refused to commit himself.

Fran wished she could appreciate the attention Jordan had lavished on her at lunchtime and was repeating tonight, but it was impossible. Jean-Claude's treachery kept flooding over her. Her only hope was to smile bravely and carry on as if nothing had happened.

The next morning she awoke with a blinding headache for her efforts. And was it surprising? she asked herself as she sat up in bed till the nausea passed; her nerves were knotted into a ball. Coming home last night Fran had desperately wanted to fling herself into Jordan's arms and tell him everything, but because of Silas's presence she hadn't. Then Jordan had been called to Reception as soon as they entered the hotel and Silas had escorted her to her room.

Today she wouldn't see Jordan till the evening; this morning he and Silas were out visiting a new clinic on the outskirts of the city and this afternoon he had a two o'clock meeting with Peter Brabben. The day stretched interminably before her. She knew she had to get out—the hotel was becoming oppressive.

Her headache eased as she stepped out into warm Paris sunshine. Without any money she couldn't go far. The hotel was in the Ecole Militaire region which wasn't too far from the Eiffel Tower, and Fran headed for the Parc du

Champ de Mars that spread out below the tower. There were hundreds of tourists wandering around and Fran had never felt so alone in her life. She had thought of trying to walk to Jean-Claude's studio but a quick perusal of a tourist map picked up from Reception put her off that idea—it was miles away. The café was closer and she could make that, but what excuse could she give to Jordan?

'Done any sketching?'

Fran jumped as she crossed the hotel foyer, and turned and give Silas a smile of relief. 'No, not this morning, but I'm going to a market this afternoon that should be far more interesting matter.'

'Then you must join me for lunch before you go,' he suggested.

Fran was already heading towards the restaurant and was pleased to have his company. 'How was the visit to the new clinic? Interesting?' What she really wanted to know was if Jordan had come back with him, but she had learned to keep her interest in him minimal when Silas was around. He appeared to have a nose for a romance and she had caught him several times studying her and Jordan curiously.

'I didn't go. I had far too much paperwork to catch up on and phone calls to make. I've been shut up in the suite all morning till hunger drove me down to the restaurant.'

Fran was momentarily puzzled by that, for hadn't she seen him across the park just now. It had been too far to call out to him but she had been sure it was him, presumed he was taking some fresh air and exercise after the visit. She must have been mistaken.

The lunch was delicious and the company easy and friendly. Silas told Fran about the power struggles going on among the corporates interested in taking over Unimet and made it sound so fascinating she found herself asking questions and actually understanding the answers.

'So the meeting with this Brabben guy from Unimet is really important this afternoon?' Fran asked over the *moules marinière*.

'*High Noon* stuff. If the drug is successful, Jordan will be in a position to make an offer for Unimet and they won't be able to stop him!' Silas told her with a twinkle in his eye.

'I'll keep my fingers crossed for you this afternoon. So tonight we will either be celebrating or drowning our sorrows.' Fran thought that a pretty crafty way of finding out what was happening later.

'Wish it was that simple. These meetings could go on for weeks. Unimet is an American company, so the meetings could continue over the Atlantic. This afternoon is the decider if they do in fact go any further. Whatever the outcome Jordan has invited Peter Brabben and his wife out to dinner tonight . . .'

Fran stifled her sigh of relief—she would be free.

'There will be just the four of you,' Silas added, sending Fran's blood-pressure soaring. He grasped her clenched fist across the rose damask tablecloth. 'Don't look so worried, you've met him already. The distinguished-looking geezer with the lavatory brush moustache and an accent as yawning as the Grand Canyon.'

Fran couldn't help giggling, Silas was so funny, but her heart lay like an exhausted brick in her chest. How could she get out of this one? She could go down with a terrible viral disease brought on by the delicious mussels she'd just eaten, but Silas had eaten the same—that idea was out. Pleading sickness was the obvious way out—pity she hadn't thought of that before she had eaten such a hearty lunch with a witness.

She wrestled with the problem as she strolled to the market, several streets from the hotel, and came to the eventual decision that Jordan came first. There was no way she could let him down, not tonight of all nights. She would have to forget Jean-Claude and put the loss of Jordan's money and her few valuables down to experience. Before she returned to England she would have to tell Jordan the truth because the money worried her; she wished he had taken it back when she had first refused it.

Her decision saddened her in a way because she wouldn't be able to help Jean-Claude. She reasoned that if she hadn't gone with Jordan to Stella's gallery she wouldn't have known of her old friend's struggles, but that didn't help very much. She *had* met up with him again and that was that.

Her spirits lifted a little as she reached the market. The atmosphere was infectious. This time she did sketch. The colourful stalls and the noisy street vendors suited her artistic temperament far more than the formal gardens below the tower. The people were Parisians, not tourists, and Fran sketched quickly and enthusiastically.

Paris loved an artist and everyone loved Fran. There was much laughter and backchat between her and the market people and she feasted on apples and hot nuts in exchange for her sketches.

Fran laughed a lot and puzzled too. She swore she saw Silas several times and once even called out, but the middle-aged man she thought was him didn't heed her call and hurried away. She vowed not to eat mussels again for lunch—she was hallucinating!

She returned to the hotel tired, but at least her nerves were finally unravelled, for a while.

'Helena!' she gasped as she entered the bedroom, letting her sketch-pad and shoulder-bag slither to her feet in dismay.

'Yes, Helena!' was the sharp retort delivered with the accuracy of a rifle shot. 'This place is like Fort Knox and what in heaven's name induced you to book yourself into here in my name? I've had one hell of a time sorting out the mess you made, convincing them *I'm* Helena Cain!' Helena was furious, Fran momentarily taken aback.

'There was a terrible crush at Reception when I arrived,' Fran explained. 'They thought I was you and I simply left it at that. I didn't think it mattered.'

'Stupid! Of course it matters!' Helena turned away from her, unpacking her make-up and setting it out on the dressing-table, pushing Fran's aside. 'If there had been a fire they would have buried the charred remains of Helena Cain, not Fran!'

'Crumbs!' Fran exclaimed sarcastically, recovering quickly. 'That would really play havoc with your life, wouldn't it?'

Her sister glowered at her. 'It's no joking matter, Fran. There are procedures to follow in a hotel like this.'

Fran sighed wearily and picked up her pad and bag. You couldn't win with Helena. 'I'm sorry,' she mumbled, though she wasn't. Her eyes dropped to Helena's heavily bandaged foot. 'How's your foot? And I thought you said you were going to have a plaster cast put on it?'

There was no placating Helena with apologies—she roared on like an Intercity express. 'Can't be doing with plasters, I persuaded them that strapping would be sufficient. I'll probably be crippled in my old age but that will be down to you, won't it?'

'Me?' Fran squeaked. 'How come it'll be my fault?'

Helena straightened herself and glared at her savagely. 'Because I had to come, didn't I? Discharged myself from hospital at my own peril to find out what chaos you are causing. The first thing I find is you've forged the hotel registration—God only knows what other misdemeanours you've perpetrated. Whatever induced Jordan to ask you to stay I'll never know. There's something going on here and I don't like it one bit!' She hobbled furiously to her suitcase on the bed, slammed it shut and almost threw it to the back of the wardrobe.

Fran stood in the middle of the room watching her with narrowed green eyes, suppressing her anger. 'There's nothing going on here, Helena, and if you are worried about my conduct I suggest you thrash it out with Jordan himself.'

'I have every intention of doing just that,' she retorted sharply. All elegance, only marred by her limp and her indignation, she swept to the door.

'I wouldn't go now if I were you,' Fran advised, and Helena's brows shot up. 'He's in a meeting with Peter Brabben and doesn't wish to be disturbed.' Fran presumed the meeting would be pretty intense and the last thing Jordan wanted was Helena and her petty grievances bursting in on him.

'My God, Fran!' Helena's lips curled in derision as she hobbled towards her. 'Have you got your feet under the table!'

'Look, I'm only thinking of you and your job, Helena,' she reasoned. 'You yourself know the strain he's under, and let me remind you it was your idea for me to come.'

'Not to take over my job...' her sister seethed.

'I'm not doing anything of the sort. Jordan asked for my help and I gave it.'

'Well, your help isn't needed any longer, sister dear,' Helena lashed cruelly. 'I'm here now and you're obsolete.'

Her words tore Fran apart. She was right, Jordan would have no further need of her now. Whatever there might have been with the charismatic head of Parry Pharmaceuticals was never to be. She slumped on the edge of the bed. She had been a fool to ever fantasise that there might have been, but she couldn't deny his kisses, couldn't convince herself that he hadn't wanted and desired her. But Helena was here now and Helena had prior claim.

'You're right,' she sighed heavily. 'But what about tonight? I was supposed to be having dinner with Jordan and Peter Brabben and his wife.'

'Dear God,' Helena huffed as she went to the bathroom. 'I've arrived in the nick of time. You and the Brabbens? Jordan must be out of his mind.'

Tears gathered at the back of Fran's eyes but she wouldn't let Helena see how badly she had upset her. 'Helena! What are you doing?' she exclaimed as she came out of the bathroom with Fran's toilet-bag.

'Packing for you. There are two flights this evening, you're sure to get a seat on one of them.' She proceeded to haul Fran's holdall from the wardrobe and Fran noticed with icy horror Helena's beautiful cocktail dresses hanging neatly in a row. It really was all over, the Paris fever, her impossible love for Jordan Parry.

'I can't go tonight!' Fran protested, leaping to her feet. She couldn't leave without seeing Jordan.

'Why not?' Helena asked, already reaching for the phone. 'Now is as good a time as any. I'm damned sure Jordan won't want you hanging around getting under everyone's feet.'

Fran ran a trembling hand across her hot forehead. The thought of never seeing Jordan again tore through her, leaving her nerves in rags. Then fate blessed her.

There were no seats available on any flights that evening or the following morning. Reprieved, Fran let her hand drop to her side.

Helena's classic features were a study in acute disappointment, a look that disturbed Fran so greatly she turned away from her and crossed to the window. Why hadn't she seen it before? Understood why Helena was so eager to be rid of her? Helena was jealous, so unsure of her relationship with Jordan that she suspected Fran was usurping her. She wasn't worried about Fran making a fool of herself jobwise, she was panicking that Jordan had turned his affections towards Fran. And had he, Fran asked uncertainly, while Helena was unavailable? Very probably.

'What are you doing now?' Fran asked as Helena picked up the phone again. Surely not the cross-Channel ferry?

'Trying to get you another room,' was the tart reply. 'We can't share this.'

'Use your common sense, Helena,' Fran interjected, turning her head back to the view out of the window. 'The hotel is jam-packed with conference people—you couldn't get a small sardine in if you tried.'

Furiously Helena slammed down the receiver. 'OK, smarty pants, you're probably right. I'll have to move into Jordan's suite, then,' she told Fran pointedly.

Slowly Fran turned back to her sister and knew for sure that her assumption of jealousy had been spot-on. That last remark had been said with one thing in mind: to remind Fran that it was Helena who held a place in Jordan Parry's heart, then and now.

They stared at each other across the room and Fran thought how much her sister must hate her. First she blamed her for taking her parents' love and now she thought she was taking her lover, except she wasn't. She had been tempted, dreamt about it, but if the crunch had come would she have gone through with it, let Jordan love her as she so ached to do? She doubted it—at the last minute her heart and her conscience would have screamed out Helena!

Helena was so beautiful, even in anger. Her figure and the way she dressed was perfection. Fran's eyes flicked to Helena's black silk négligé draped over the back of the heavy brocade chair and knew her own torn yellow nightie, rolled up under her pillow, was no match for that. Jordan would take one look at Helena and forget the existence of her little sister.

Helena glanced impatiently at her watch, shot herself an admiring glance in the mirror and said, 'He'll be through with Brabben now and if he isn't he should be. It's getting late and there are things to be arranged.'

Fran breathed a hesitant sigh of relief after she had gone. Perhaps it was as well she was moving into the suite with Jordan. She couldn't stand another minute of her company. She bit back the pain of thinking of the two of them in that elegant old suite. It was all over, her love for Jordan a wretched waste of effort. She went through to run a bath, and bit so determinedly on her lip that she nearly drew blood. The tears came then, tears for her loss and a love that was hopeless.

To her surprise Helena was back in the bedroom in next to no time.

'It looks as if we'll have to suffer each other after all,' Helena called out. 'Jordan regretfully informed me that Silas has the other bedroom of the suite.'

Soaking in the bath, Fran clamped a hot wet hand to her mouth to stifle a sob of sheer pleasure. He had lied, Jordan had lied! Silas had a room only a few doors along from hers. Jordan didn't want Helena in the suite!

'Get a move on, Fran.' Helena pounded on the door. 'You're not going anywhere, so quit hogging the bathroom I have to get ready.'

Fran eased herself out of the bath without washing. Wrapped in a towel, she stood dripping in the doorway. 'I—I expect he's pleased to see you back,' she fished.

'Delighted,' she clipped, her back to Fran, swishing dresses backwards and forwards along the wardrobe rail. 'I must say he looks worn out. I've told him to get some rest, not that he will heed my advice. The man is a human dynamo. Hopefully I can take some of the strain off his shoulders now that I'm here. Quite a man, isn't he?' she asked rhetorically, selecting a lapis lazuli blue silk dress and flinging it across the bed. 'Pure virility with a capital "V",' she trilled happily.

And you're pure bitch with a capital 'B', Fran thought miserably as she went back into the bathroom to dry herself properly. Jordan might have lied about the bedroom but he had accepted Helena back with open arms, and it was obvious she had slipped back into her role of perfect secretary and was accompanying Jordan and the Brabbens to dinner. Well, one good thing had come out of the whole painful mess: she was free to meet Jean-Claude as arranged. She would devote her attentions to helping him and try to forget this lead weight in her chest.

'Where the hell are you going?' Helena challenged as Fran was dressing later, the usual jeans, sweater and comfortable trainers for the long walk ahead of her.

'Out,' Fran answered facetiously. The room was heady with her sister's expensive perfume, the designer label of Helena's exotic evening dress prominently displayed on the bed adding insult to Fran's meagre appearance. Helena was sitting by the window putting another layer of glossy nail-polish over her nails.

'I can see that, but where and with whom?' came the uninterested question.

'Only a café. I ran into an old schoolfriend the other day. I didn't think I'd get the chance to meet up with her again so I rang her while you were with Jordan. We arranged to have a meal together this evening.' It was partly true, a little gender-bending, that was all. No reason for Helena to know the old schoolfriend was a male.

'Bit of a remote coincidence meeting up with an old friend in Paris, isn't it?'

Fran eyed her curiously but she was studying her nails hard—she'd simply been making conversation and wasn't suspicious, as Fran had thought. No, it was Fran acting suspiciously, looking for problems looming up all the time.

'Stranger things have happened, Helena,' she murmured and left it at that.

The evening was pleasantly warm and the walk undaunting. It was quite a way but Fran was glad to stretch her legs and hopefully clear her mind. There was nothing she could do about Jordan but try and live with the pain inside her. In a way it helped knowing she was going to try and do something for Jean-Claude. She decided she would not make a big issue over her stolen belongings—no point anyway, she had little chance of recovering them—but she would certainly try to persuade him to seek professional help because to have done what he did he must have been pretty desperate.

'The Café La Rochelle? Yes, I know it, but it isn't the sort of place a nice young lady like yourself should frequent,' an old Parisian gentleman told her when she stopped him for directions. He gave them reluctantly.

Fran wasn't surprised to hear that Jean-Claude's café was one of ill repute. She hadn't expected he would arrange to meet her in anywhere swish, not under his dire circumstances. The Café La Rochelle sounded right up his alley.

It *was* up an alley, a narrow dingy walkway that opened into a small, pretty courtyard. It would have been delightful with very little expenditure, potted geraniums and a coat of white paint, but the owner had neglected it badly. The wooden shutters hung broken and unpainted and the curtains at the greasy windows were stained brown with years of nicotine.

Fran stepped into the gloomy interior, and almost lost her courage and stepped smartly out again. Jean-Claude wasn't there, and her first thought was that she had been stood up, but she asked the dowdy young girl behind the coffee-stained counter the time and if she knew Jean-Claude. It was past eight and yes, she knew Jean-Claude, but it was a little early for him, he'd be in later. Yes, definitely, he came to the café every night. Suddenly the girl tilted her head to one side.

'Are you the English friend of Jean-Claude's— Fran?' she asked.

Fran's heart slumped. 'Yes, yes, I am. Did he leave a message for me?' Perhaps he couldn't make it; her feet throbbed at the thought of the long walk back if he couldn't.

'No message.' The girl smiled. 'He mentioned you were coming, that is all. Said you were a good friend from England.'

Well, that was something at least. It seemed Jean-Claude intended coming. Resigned to being kept waiting, Fran sat in the corner by the greasy window and the smelly curtains. She'd come far enough and she wasn't about to storm out in a huff because he was late. She desperately wanted a coffee but had no money to pay for it, so concentrated on a game of dominoes being played by a group of old men at the next table.

Gradually the café filled up with younger people and the old men got up and shuffled into a back room. Fran's eyes searched the knots of people for Jean-Claude but couldn't see him.

She moved further into the corner of the table when a group of young men and girls thumped themselves down beside her, laughing and shrieking. Someone put a heavy rock disc on a cassette player and the noise thumped deafeningly in Fran's ears. She shifted in her seat uneasily. The air was becoming thick and heavy with tobacco smoke when the dark-haired girl sitting next to her leaned closer and offered her a cigarette.

'No—no, thank you. I don't smoke,' she told the girl.

The rest of her scruffy companions were quick to pick up her accent.

'You are English, yes?'

'Jean-Claude's friend?'

Fran's head spun with the questions fired at her. Their words and jibes and bad breath crowded in on her and her stomach writhed into knots. It had been a mistake to come, a bad mistake. There was no sign of Jean-Claude and she was desperately afraid he wasn't coming at all. She tried to stand up.

'I must go.'

'No, no.' The youth next to her wrenched at her arm, forced her back into her seat. 'You are too beautiful to leave us.' The others laughed again. 'You will stay and we will teach you how to live.' He touched her face with filthy fingers and Fran shuddered. 'No, no, *chérie*, do not be afraid. We will not hurt you. Here, try this, it will make you smile.' He moved a glass of whisky to her lips and Fran cried out, shaking her head, terror clutching at her with a fearsome horror. She had to get out—and then suddenly the youth seemed to leap a foot in the air and landed on the floor, his chair toppling over his legs.

Fran lurched back against the window with shock and then she was being grabbed by her shoulders and hauled out from behind the table. The room and the protesting crowd at the table spun around her and she cried out and struggled to be free.

'Hold still, for God's sake!'

Hands grabbed at her, pulling her this way and that, but one pair of hands dominated, held her with a strength and power above all others. Fran twisted her flushed face up to her assailant and her blood drained, leaving her weak and dizzy.

'Jordan! Jordan, what...?'

She had never been so pleased to see anyone in her life and clung to him. He wasn't attacking her but saving her—at least that was what she thought. Till she saw the whiteness of his face and the fire of fury in his eyes and then she was more afraid of him than the youths who had been hassling her. His grip on her tightened murderously and he shoved her with such force towards the door, she let out a cry.

'Jordan, please, you're hurting me!'

'I'll kill you when I get you outside!' he grated furiously.

She didn't doubt it.

CHAPTER SEVEN

JORDAN didn't speak or let Fran go till they were out of the alleyway and on the street.

'Charming friends you have!' he growled at last, brushing down his dinner-jacket with both hands.

Fran rubbed her arms where he'd held her so brutally. 'They aren't my friends. I've never seen them before in my life.'

'You looked pretty chummy to me.'

Jordan's car was parked at the kerbside, the motor purring softly, the chauffeur at the wheel, eyes discreetly ahead. Jordan, his hand on her elbow, steered her towards it.

Suddenly Fran rebelled. She needed fresh air, not the stuffy confines of the back of a car.

Embarrassment powered her down the street. Suppose she had been with Jean-Claude and Jordan had done that, stormed into the café and rushed her out as if she were a juvenile delinquent? She heard Jordan's voice behind her, instructing David to drive round the block and calling out to her to wait.

He caught up with her as she blazed down the street. Confused, she turned to him. 'How did you know where I was? And why aren't you at dinner with Brabben, and where is Helena?'

The heated questions came out in a rush but went unanswered. There were people on the pavement, brushing past them, forcing Jordan to step away from her. Impatiently he reached out and took her arm, forced her across the wide pavement and into a quiet, narrow street. They walked for a few yards then he urged her into a dark doorway. Fran tripped on the step, he grabbed at her and then they were in each other's arms.

Jordan held her so fiercely she could hardly breathe, and she gulped at air and clung to him, so very glad to feel the warmth and security of him protecting her. Though embarrassed, she shuddered to think what might have happened if he hadn't rescued her from that loathsome place.

She lifted her head to speak but no words materialised. His mouth crushed hers and she slumped against him, her legs melting with a strange mixture of relief and love.

His kiss was long and passionate and so very nearly out of control. He pressed her hard into the cold stone wall of the doorway, his breathing heavy, his body strained against her thin, quavering figure.

Then with a supreme effort that left him drained and trembling slightly he tore his lips from hers. She clung to him fiercely, afraid to let him go.

He took a small step back from her, covered her hands with his and prised them from the lapels of his jacket. He smiled down at her, a smile she could only just see in the dim light from a street lamp.

'I'm sorry.' She smoothed the lapels with her long, artistic fingers. 'I didn't realise what I was doing. I—I was just so glad to see you,' she husked.

'Why did you try to run away from me, then?' He tilted her chin to look into her face.

'I was ashamed...' She gave a small shrug. 'Embarrassed that you had caught me in that café.'

'You were waiting for Jean-Claude, weren't you?'

She couldn't look at him, stared down at the litter-strewn ground, didn't answer.

'I told you not to see him again, Fran—you disobeyed me,' he said quietly.

A spark of anger flared and died. 'I—I had to, Jordan.'

'You still care for him so very much.' His voice was dull and low.

Fran looked up sharply, confused by his tone. 'He needed me,' she said simply.

He gripped her arms. 'The truth, Fran,' he rasped thickly. 'Do you still love him?'

'No...no.' She shook herself free. 'I never did! I mean I thought I did when we were at college, but it was only a crush. I realised that when I didn't lose any sleep over him when he went back to France.'

'So why now, why the sudden urge to renew the friendship——?'

'Look, none of this was my doing in the first place,' Fran protested. 'It was Stella's idea——'

'It wasn't Stella's idea to entertain him in your bedroom, was it? You wanted to see him again, and it's why you're here tonight...'

'Yes, it's why I'm here tonight,' Fran retorted. 'I had to come, Jordan... He needed me...he's in trouble...'

'And you thought his need was greater than mine?' he asked harshly, his metallic eyes glittering wildly. 'I shouldn't be here, Fran Cain. I walked out on a dinner engagement with a very important man tonight, jeopardised my company's future because I was terrified of what might happen to you in that place. Do you know the Café La Rochelle is known for its drug connections?'

Fran shook her head. 'Of course I didn't——'

'And I don't suppose you knew Jean-Claude was a drug addict——'

'Of course I did!' Fran shouted back. 'That's why I agreed to meet him!'

'You what?' He was almost shaking with rage and his hands bit into her arms again. 'You...you don't...'

Fran's whole body stiffened rigidly and the blood ran from her face. 'You don't think... Oh,

Jordan, you don't think I take drugs as well, do you?' she croaked.

He let her go, abruptly. 'No—no, of course not. I'm sorry, Fran—it's just that you shocked me when you said you knew Jean-Claude's problem. I didn't think you did.'

'But how did *you* know?' Fran frowned.

'Stella told me when she came to see me about the prints. I didn't think anything of it till I saw him coming from your room.'

'You thought the worst,' Fran said bitterly. 'You thought I was involved with drugs?'

'No, that wasn't what was on my mind,' he said quietly.

Fran's mouth twisted angrily, guessing precisely what had been on his mind. 'I don't know what's worse, your thinking I'm some sort of addict or some sort of tart.' She tried to move out of the doorway but he barred her way with his arm.

'I thought neither of those things, Fran,' he told her steadily. 'I was worried about you, that's all.'

'You think I can't look after myself?' She lifted her chin stubbornly.

'Tonight was a good example of how you look after yourself, was it?' he questioned sarcastically.

'I wasn't in any kind of danger, Jordan,' she argued. 'No one can make me do something I don't want to do.' A frown creased her brow. 'How did you know I was there, anyway?'

'When Silas saw you leaving the hotel, he followed you because he knew I'd be worried. He phoned me when you arrived at the café, and I knew that La Rochelle is known for drug connections...'

'Silas followed me to the café?' Fran echoed, her eyes saucer-like with disbelief. Her mind spun back to the day. 'He's been following me all day, hasn't he? I wasn't imagining things after all. He was in the park and the market. You made him follow me?'

'I was worried——'

'How dare you?' Fran cried furiously. 'How dare you do such a thing?'

'For you own good, Fran!'

'My own good! You were thinking of yourself, Jordan Parry!' she flamed. 'You don't trust me further than you can throw me. All you were thinking of was your damned conference and your company. You were terrified of a scandal. Jordan Parry's little helper involved in drugs——'

'Don't be ridiculous——'

'And don't tell me not to be ridiculous!' She pushed his arm away from the doorway and stepped into the comparative brightness of the street. 'I'm going back to the café,' she called out behind her. 'I'm going to meet someone who *does* trust me, someone who needs me. And don't you dare follow me.' She turned to add weight to her words. 'Don't you dare!'

She turned and started to run, but got nowhere. He seemed to bear down on her from a great height, wrenched at her arm and swung her round.

'What have I got to say or do to get through to you, you wretch?' he breathed heavily. 'You are not going back to that café and you can forget Jean-Claude Lafarge's existence.'

'No way!' she cried and lifted her hand to strike him but he caught her wrists, and before she could protest his mouth came down hard on hers in an impassioned kiss that knocked the fight from her.

'I'll do that again and again till you decide to behave yourself,' he told her brittly when he finally released her. 'Now we are going back to the hotel——'

'No!' she stated breathlessly. 'I can't, Jordan. I'm going back to the café to wait for Jean-Claude. You don't understand.' She swallowed hard. 'He needs my help. He stole from me because——'

'He what?'

Fran lowered her eyes. She hadn't meant that to come out. 'He...that night in my room...after he'd gone I found he'd taken the money you gave me... I'd—I'd meant to give it back to you. I hadn't spent any of it. He took it and my watch and a bracelet——'

'My God!' Jordan exhaled. 'And still you want to help him.'

'It was a cry for help...'

Jordan struggled to hold his temper—muscles on his face were taut with fury. 'Fran, he stole to feed his habit. The man is a junkie...'

The whole evening seemed to close in on Fran, wrapping her in a fiery ball of fury. She exploded out of it. 'You call yourself a doctor? Jean-Claude needs help, not labels!' Her eyes narrowed suspiciously. 'I told you before you haven't a scrap of humanity in you. You don't care for anyone but yourself. Drugs are more profitable than people——'

'Shut up, Fran!' His voice rang loud and clear in the deserted dark street and Fran tensed. He was a man without feeling and she didn't know how she had thought she loved him.

'I hate you, Jordan Parry!' she spat.

It was as if she had driven a stake through his heart. The pain in his eyes was more than Fran could bear. She saw it all then, the reason they were confronting each other so wildly in this anonymous side-street of Paris. He shouldn't be here, he should be running his company, her spinning thoughts reasoned, but he wasn't, he'd risked all to help her. Suddenly she didn't want to see any more, the paleness of his features, the exhaustion etched forever more into the lines around his strained eyes.

She turned and ran, shame and humiliation spurring her recklessly on. He called her name once, as if torn from his heart, and she faltered, her legs suddenly too heavy to move. Her foot slithered into the gutter, twisted and she sprawled into the road, lights spinning around her like a merry-go-round.

He cradled her in his arms in the back of the car and she cried softly. Her body ached with the release of the tension and her foot throbbed angrily. She thought of Helena in the very same predicament days before—but she hadn't had Jordan to comfort her. She tried not to think of her sister and felt dizzy with the effort.

'I'm sorry I said all those——'

'Hush,' he warned softly, squeezing her shoulders, and Fran got the message. David, the chauffeur, drove stoically through the streets of Paris to the sanctity of the Clermont.

Jordan helped her to his suite, which was deserted. She lay exhausted on the sofa while he made several phone calls then he checked her over.

'You've just wrenched your foot, no bones broken.'

'Jordan, please forgive me. I said some wicked things to you tonight and I regret them very much.'

He crossed to the bar and poured two brandies. 'They sounded as if they came from the heart.'

'I was angry with you, Jordan,' she admitted in a hushed whisper. 'You didn't seem to care about Jean-Claude. You don't know him the way I do. When I first realised what was wrong with him I was shocked, repulsed too, but when I thought of how he used to be, all that talent going to waste, I wanted to help. He needs proper counselling. He's still grieving for his brother. He can't help the way he is——'

There was an ear-splitting crash as Jordan slammed a brandy glass down on the top of the bar.

'For God's sake, Fran, leave it alone. Don't try to lecture me on a subject you know little about. You can only help someone if they want to help themselves. Do you understand that?'

Fran nodded miserably and took the brandy he offered her. 'Yes, of course I understand, but you see in a way he *was* asking for help; his stealing was a cry for help.'

'He stole to buy drugs, Fran,' he told her tightly. 'He didn't give you a thought. If he wants help he can walk into any number of centres in Paris and get counselling.'

'Maybe——'

'Drop it, Fran, before I lose my temper.' He swallowed his brandy and Fran gulped at hers.

'I only wanted to help,' Fran murmured, staring blindly into her empty glass.

'If you want to do your Nightingale act I'll take you to my father's hospice in England and you can comfort those who have no second chance at life.'

The brandy she had gulped so quickly and the catastrophic evening finally hit Fran's stomach and she lurched to the bathroom, nausea clutching her insides into a knot. Jordan was immediately behind her and held her head as she was sick.

'I'm sorry...' she gasped and choked. 'Oh, Jordan...' She clutched at her stomach, strangely unembarrassed by her predicament.

'I'm sorry too, Fran,' he said very quietly. 'I've been hard on you tonight but sometimes you can be so obstinate. Now hold on to the edge of the sink for support and I'll get you some water from the bar.'

She did as she was told and when he came back he supported her while she brushed her teeth and rinsed her mouth. She drank some of the sparkling water and felt better. She sat on the bathroom stool and watched while he ran a bath for her.

'Jordan, tell me about tonight. I don't mean the café. What happened with the Brabbens and Helena?'

He sat on the edge of the bath and looked at her. 'Helena.' He smiled wryly. 'Helena has taken them out to dinner. I couldn't believe it when she turned up this afternoon. I got the distinct impression she thought I'd gone out of my mind.' Fran smiled. 'She stepped in as if she'd never been away. I was expecting you this evening, but she arrived instead. Then Silas panicked me with the news that you were going out.' He shook his head and grinned. 'Poor Silas, he had one hell of a job keeping up with you.'

Fran laughed. 'Did he get back all right?'

'Took a taxi to the restaurant to join Helena and the Brabbens.'

'You should be with them, Jordan,' Fran whispered.

'Some things are more important,' he murmured. He moved round the spacious bathroom, pouring a milky essence into the steaming water, laying out a pile of fluffy towels for her. Fran watched, her heart racing wildly. He must care, she thought happily, he had risked everything for her tonight. He should be buying out Unimet but here he was running a bath for an obstinate wretch with his dinner-jacket sleeves pushed up over his elbows. She ached with love for him.

Before she knew what was happening he skilfully eased her out of her jeans and sweater, swept her into his arms and carefully lowered her naked body into the warm water. Fran trembled as the silky water enfolded her and held on to the sides for support.

'I didn't see you test this water with your elbow,' she tried to joke to cover her shyness at sitting naked in the bath in front of him, the water barely covering her midriff. 'I—I might be lobster-red when I get out.'

'You won't be.' He smiled down at her.

'Don't leave me!' she cried as he moved towards the door. 'I . . . I don't want to be alone.' Suddenly she felt very peculiar, shaking inside.

'I'll join you in a minute. I'm going to get out of these clothes.' He disappeared, leaving Fran with every pulse racing at the thought of him joining her in the bath.

She was vaguely disappointed when five minutes later he returned in his bathrobe, his hair dripping wet from showering in the other bathroom.

He took the largest of the bathsheets, and hauling her to her feet he wrapped it round her and pulled her against him. He stood her on the rug and she stayed in his arms, snuggled up in the towel, her cheek resting against his shoulder. He pressed warm kisses on the top of her head and Fran wanted to stay this way forever. Warm and safe and loved.

'Jordan,' she murmured languidly, 'remember earlier I said I hated you?' His body against hers momentarily tensed. 'Well . . . well, it was a s-slip of the tongue. I . . . I meant to say I loved you.' She was unsure then, afraid she had admitted to something he couldn't equal. Helena pressed in on her thoughts and again the sickness rose inside her. She shouldn't have said anything when he only cared for her sister; but he didn't, she reminded herself—he cared for her, tonight had proved it.

His body was now relaxed and supple next to hers and then he said it, softly and huskily. 'I love you too, morning primrose.'

Tears of pure happiness sprang to her eyes as she looked up at him. He smiled and lowered his mouth to hers, parting her rapturous lips and holding her safe and secure in his arms. Weak and dizzy with the desire rising like tidal water in her heart, she felt him lift her easily and effortlessly into his arms.

The bed was already turned down and he slipped her between the cool sheets, whipping off the damp towel as he did so. He covered her up to her chin and bent down and kissed her mouth.

Wriggling her hands free of the covers, she clung to him, sobbing out his name. He held her for a while, kissing her lips, her throat, the hollows beneath her ears, and then he drew away from her, painfully, as if it was the last thing he wanted to do.

'Why, Jordan, why?' she whispered. He wanted her, she knew, his kisses had grown deeper, more passionate, his body rigid with the need building up inside him, and she had wanted him too, with an ache that longed for release, a sweet pain that had twisted her body convulsively beneath the sheets.

'You need sleep more than you need me at the moment,' he husked and pulled the covers back up to her chin. 'Sleep, my darling primrose, we have all the time in the world.'

The ache eased then, the desire floated away as she smiled up at him. She loved him for that, his concern, his love, his respect. Her eyelids grew heavy. How right he was, as always. He seemed to know her through and through, had seen the willingness but sensed the fatigue. She slept, secure in the knowledge that he would be waiting when she awoke.

It was barely light when she snapped open her eyes. Her mouth was dry and her body ached. She sat up gingerly and put her twisted foot to the ground. It passed the test, and with a sigh of relief she got up and went to the window. It was just getting light but there was no sign of life outside on the boulevard.

Shivering, she opened the wardrobe and slipped on one of Jordan's freshly laundered shirts. She wrapped it tightly around her, trying to bring him back to her.

Where was he? she wondered. Icicles of fear slithered down her spine. Had he gone to Helena? She bit her lip as a punishment for her doubt. He had said he loved her. Her, not Helena.

He lay asleep in the other bedroom. A full bottle of Scotch stood unopened on the bedside table as if he'd anticipated a sleepless night. Fran was relieved he hadn't touched it.

She stood by the double bed looking down on his handsome features at rest. His hair, so curly-crumpled, still looked damp from the night before and he had a crease down the side of his face where he had lain on it. Had he stirred when she'd opened the door? Did he know she was standing over him, adoration flooding from her every pore?

Softly Fran moved to the other side of the bed. Dared she? Dared she slip into bed beside him? Just to be near him, feel his warmth next to her. He moaned slightly as she lowered her body carefully into the space next to him, wriggled herself under the covers.

She lay there, stiff, almost too terrified to breathe in case he woke suddenly. Would he throw her out if he did? Her breath quickened at the frightening thought and then she calmed down. He was here, wasn't he? Not with Helena but here ... waiting for her.

Rolling on to her side, she faced him. He was lying on his back, naked. She couldn't resist the impulse to touch, to kiss, to run her lips over the hardness of his skin, to brush her soft cheek across the roughness of the dark hair on his chest.

Why do men have nipples? she mused. She would ask him some time—he was a doctor, he must know everything. Were they sensitive to stimulus, as sensitive as hers were now, pressed hard against his side? She ran the tip of her tongue over his to see, and her green eyes widened as another moan escaped his lips.

She was gentler in her exploration from then on. Smoothing her palms over the flatness of his stomach, tracing her fingers over hard muscle, thrilling at her touch and the thought of her wickedness and daring. To be touching this man's body in such a way and not afraid or caring because it was so very right.

He slept on, unaware of her sensual exploration of discovery. His thighs were muscular, bigger than they appeared in the narrow trousers of his suit, and... Oh, my God! She drew her hand away as if it had touched burning coals. His body trembled and, startled, Fran looked up to his face. He was laughing, a deep, silent laugh. He pulled her towards him and crushed her against his nakedness, knocking the breath from her.

'What a delicious way to be woken.' His mouth sought hers, urgently.

'I didn't mean to wake you,' she uttered weakly when they paused for breath.

'Funny girl,' he growled softly in her ear. 'How much longer did you think I could stand it?' He rolled her on to her back. 'Let me look at my morning primrose. Ah, yes, as beautiful and as fresh as ever. Did you sleep well?'

She smiled up at him. 'I could have slept better,' she murmured suggestively.

'You will, later—much later.'

Her smile faded as his hand slid under her shirt to her breasts. He cupped and teased them till she cried out in painful ecstasy.

'Am I hurting you?' He lowered his mouth to soothe her satin-smooth flesh and her body arched against him, her skin tremulous against the hardness of him.

'No, it's wonderful,' she husked. She tried to free herself of his shirt, to feel every part of his body on her own heated skin, but he stilled her hands and guided them to his hips.

'Leave the shirt, I like it, it's sexy. Parts of you I can see and parts I can only touch.'

Her hands smoothed over him as his travelled over hers. She felt dizzy with her love for him, completely uninhibited in her passion. That was the way he made her feel—proud of her body and unafraid to adore his.

His body grew more and more restless and when his hand stroked the inside of her thighs she grew restless with him. She moved against his hand till her desire grew to such proportions she was nearly delirious with need.

'I love you, my primrose.' He eased away from her to see the effect his words and the rhythmic movement of his hand had on her lovely features.

Her head thrashed from side to side on the white pillow and she murmured fretfully, 'I love you too, Jordan.'

He moved across her and she cried out and clutched at him, half afraid, half crazy with her need.

'You're too wonderful for words,' she gasped as he eased against her, gently at first then powered more fiercely by an urgency that was unstoppable.

Her nails grazed his back and she cried out a muffled cry of apology. 'I'm sorry... Oh, Jordan...'

His mouth silenced her and she clung to him, moved with him, soared with him.

'How I love you... Don't let me go, Jordan... don't lose me.'

'Never,' he bit out his passion, his breath harsh and grating. 'I'll never lose you. You're mine forever.'

She woke him with her kisses, sweet warm kisses as the Paris sun streamed through the windows.

He blinked open his smoky grey eyes and smiled at her. She drew away from him and opened her mouth to speak but he clamped a hand firmly over her mouth before she could utter a word.

'Please,' he implored, 'please, not another word.' He wrapped his arms around her so tightly she couldn't have spoken a word if she had tried. 'Never before have I made love to a woman who talked non-stop all the way through it.'

Fran giggled and managed to squeeze out a few words. 'You haven't been around much, have you?'

He sounded mock incredulous. 'You mean there are more like you around?'

She laughed against his chin and nipped it with her teeth. 'I wouldn't know about that, would I? Is it so unusual, then, to talk while making love?'

'That sounds like a loaded question, one I don't wish to expand on.'

'I'm glad.' She smiled. 'I wasn't probing your love-life, honestly. I'm sorry if I talked a lot.' She snuggled against him. 'I was excited and nervous, you see. I always chatter when I'm excited.'

She looked up at the man she loved and adored and thought she had never been happier in her life. She linked her arms around his neck and very, very slowly kissed him on the mouth till she felt the rise of his passion and the quickening of his breath. She promised, very softly in his ear, not to utter a word, and with great difficulty she kept her promise, for a whole thirty minutes.

'Coffee, darling?'

'I'd love some,' Fran murmured contentedly as she stretched lazily on a sea of happiness. She bunched the pillow under her head and watched Jordan slip on his bathrobe.

'You have a lovely body,' she commented.

'I should have said that.'

'Don't be so vain!' she laughed.

'You know what I mean. *You* have a lovely body.' He was laughing as he went out of the door, leaving it ajar.

Fran lay there in a dream, still not able to believe that Jordan loved her. She touched her love-sated body gingerly. Had she dreamt all this, imagined it? No, it was all true. She floated with happiness, and drifted off to sleep.

She awoke to a knock on the door—Jordan was gone.

'You didn't come back to the room last night, Fran. Can I take it that you spent the night here with Jordan?' Helena's voice was harsher than usual, clipped with a bitterness that reached down to the very soul of Fran's being.

'Helena!' Fran gasped.

Helena closed in on Fran like a man-eating spider with a defenceless fly trapped in its web. 'You little tramp.' She almost choked with rage. 'You silly little bitch.'

'It's not like that, Helena!' Fran protested. Oh, please don't let her spoil it, don't let her sever the magic. She reached over the side of the bed for Jordan's shirt, which had somehow found its way to the floor. She slipped it round her shoulders. 'Don't call me names, Helena. I'm not a tramp. Jordan and I love each other.'

Helena gave out a hysterical laugh. 'I've no doubt you've fallen for him—what woman hasn't?—but him, love you? You've got to be out of your mind.'

'He said——'

'He said he loved you?' Helena crowed sarcastically. 'You're greener than a cabbage and

half as intelligent if you believe that, sister dear.'
She towered above Fran sitting nervously on the
edge of the bed. 'You idiot, Fran. Don't you
know when you're being used——?'

'I'm not being used!' Fran hissed back, beads
of perspiration breaking out on her forehead. She
hadn't been used, she hadn't! How could she
make Helena understand that Jordan really loved
her?

'You were available when I wasn't,' Helena
lashed spitefully. 'I know Jordan, Fran, I know
the sort of woman he needs, and you aren't it.
Can't you see the pressure he's under with this
conference? He needs me, and when it's all over
it will be me he turns too, me he'll want to marry!'

'Marry!' Fran cried in anguish.

Helena laughed again. 'Poor Fran, you can't
see it, can you? Jordan Parry is a man of substance—what the hell can you offer him but a bit
of light relief? You're a scatterbrain, not to be
taken seriously. I can give him everything and
more.'

'Shut up, Helena! I won't listen to any more.
Jordan and I——'

'Light relief. That's all you were to him, Fran.
If I hadn't had that accident I'd be wearing that
shirt now!'

The cloth seemed to sear her skin, burnt her
flesh with a painful intensity. She stared wildly
at her sister, not wanting to believe but finding

every word she had said striking fear and uncertainty into her. Fran bit her lip, battled with a flood of tears, tried to reason that Helena was wrong. She wanted Jordan to rush in and tell Helena to get out, but he didn't. After their night of love he had left her. The truth dawned then, crashed in on her senses till her head reeled. Helena was right, she'd been a bit of light relief to ease Jordan's tension. Helena was back now and he didn't need her any more.

'Walk out with your pride still intact,' Helena advised unexpectedly softly.

Fran stood up and without another word to her sister she walked out—but not with pride, that was the furthest thought from her mind. She left Helena standing in the bedroom, and left the suite with her life in ruins and her heart bleeding painfully.

CHAPTER EIGHT

'THAT trip to Paris didn't do you much good, luvvy. You've been back a week now and I haven't seen that sunny smile of yours since before you left.'

Fran smiled affectionately at her boss. Solly was shifting cases of wine under the counter and Fran was checking them off on a delivery sheet. It was the first time he'd mentioned her trip and was probably a hint for her to buck her ideas up—a sullen barmaid wasn't good for business.

'Oh, it was a bit of a disappointment, that's all,' she told him. 'I delivered Helena's briefcase to her boss and kicked around for a few days. To be honest I'm glad to be back where the action is. Paris isn't all that it's cracked up to be.'

The wine bar was gradually filling up for the evening trade and Fran glanced around at the flushed faces, the false smiles and listened to the raised voices all competing for air-space. This was the action, was it? If only they knew what she had been through in Paris. She'd been accused of being a spy, been robbed by a drug-crazed artist, fallen in love, had her heart shredded and nearly murdered her sister! Modesty Blaise had nothing on her.

Fran had swept out of the Hotel Clermont on a tidal wave of hysteria. In her frenzied state of grief she had imagined Jordan sprinting across the tarmac as her plane taxied down the runway, demanding for her to be handed out as he couldn't live without her. Hot tears had scorched her eyes as the aircraft soared into the skies without any such hitch occurring.

He could have done something, she had reasoned a hundred times since. He could have come to the hotel bedroom while she had packed, he could have phoned to say Helena was wrong and he loved only her. His silence had been the confirmation that Helena had been right. She had been used. His murmured words of love had been a tissue of lies. She had been humiliated by him and by her sister. And to add to that she'd had to rely on Helena to organise her flight home *and* borrow money from her to get to the airport.

'A bottle of Chablis and two glasses, Fran, and cheer up, old beanie, you look very down in the dumps.'

Fran forced a smile for Matthew and hastily dispensed with the cork of the bottle. *This* she could do without, she grumbled to herself, opening bottles of French wine which reminded her bitterly of Jordan and plotting how to refuse the invitation she anticipated coming from the persistent Matthew Bates.

'How about this party tonight after you've finished here? It's at Annabelle's flat and there'll be the usual crowd. I'd really like you to come.'

Common sense told her she should accept his invitation. That was the cure for a broken heart, wasn't it? To throw yourself back into the deep end of life. Sink or swim. Matthew was nice enough, but he wasn't Jordan and Fran's heart ached for only him.

'Sorry, Matt.' She smiled sweetly. 'I have to bath the alligator tonight.'

'You and that ridiculous alligator!' He laughed, well used to her eccentric excuses. 'Can't you stay in to wash your hair like other girls?' He took his wine and glasses and left her to her misery.

And misery it was. Fran had never experienced anything like it in her life. It was mental torture and a physical pain in her heart. Everything she came into contact with reminded her of Jordan. The paintings in the gallery reminded her of the Delphine Gallery and how he had leaned over her shoulder to look at the lovely apple orchard water-colour. Primroses were flowering in Helena's window-boxes—had he called Helena his morning primrose? Of course he hadn't, she was more his hybrid tea-rose. And wine, she was surrounded by it, a constant reminder of the first time she met him and he'd thought her a little mad for not liking French wine. Now, every time she uncorked a bottle it was like pulling the plug on her heart and draining away her life blood.

After closing time, she helped Solly tidy up and then they left together in his Jaguar. He always drove her home though it was out of his way, but Solly was a father of three daughters and he wouldn't allow them to make their own way home at this hour, so what was good enough for his own was good enough for Fran.

'You should have gone to the party with Matthew tonight,' he said as they drove along the King's Road.

'You don't miss much, do you, Solly?' Fran said wryly.

'No, I don't.' He grinned. 'You should have gone. Matt is a bit of a twit but he'd treat you all right, not like this Paris fly-by-night who's twisting your heart up.'

Fran lowered her eyes to her fingers, wrapped around themselves in her lap. She'd not said much about her painful trip to Paris, but Solly knew—he had an intuitive mind. 'It shows, does it?' she murmured.

'I should say so. Proper little tragedy queen you are. Chalky white face, tear-brimming eyes...'

Fran couldn't help but laugh. 'You're exaggerating, Solly. I don't look that bad, do I?'

'You look awful. Put off a case of Algerian tonight, you did,' he joked.

'Huh, it doesn't take much to put that off!' she said grinning back at him.

They laughed together and then Solly's kind round face became more serious. 'If there's anything I can do, Fran, just ask.' He pulled into the curving terrace of Regency houses and stopped outside Helena's ground-floor flat. 'If you want to talk about it, bend my ear, don't bottle it up.'

Biting back the tears, Fran turned to him. 'One day perhaps, Solly. It's too painful now.' Impulsively she reached over and hugged him and kissed his cheek. 'Thanks for being such a super boss and a good friend, Solly.' She got out of the car, slammed the door and waved him down the street.

'Back to your old tricks,' a voice grated behind her.

Ashen-faced, Fran swung round to see Jordan coming down the steps of the house towards her. A week had changed him. He looked thinner, his face pale, his smoke-grey eyes dark-ringed with strain and anguish. None of her doing—she'd read the business pages of the dailies; from Paris the Parry Pharmaceutical entourage had flown on to Chicago to continue their talks with Unimet. No, he hadn't lost any sleep over her.

'What do you mean by that?' she asked, but knew. He had seen her kissing Solly.

'A bit old for you, isn't he?' He stopped in front of her on the pavement. 'On reflection I think Jean-Claude was more your mark.'

Fran clenched her fists to her sides. She had imagined this moment, imagined that if ever they did meet again she would throw herself into his arms and somehow everything would be all right again. What a hopeless dream.

'Solly is my boss,' she told him, and he raised a brow and it reminded her that *he* was Helena's boss. 'Successful trip?' she asked politely. They were like strangers.

'Very. Arrived back this evening. I've just brought Helena from the airport.'

'Yes, yes, you would, wouldn't you?' she murmured. With a shrug of her shoulders she turned away. 'Well, goodnight, then.'

He spun her to face him, his eyes hard and metallic. 'Is that all you can say? Well, goodnight, then! You walked out on me, Fran, just walked out without an explanation.'

'Was one necessary?' Fran bit back. How could he even mention such a thing when he was on the verge of marrying her sister? 'I know when I'm not needed any more.'

'Not needed any more?' he echoed.

She levelled her eyes at him. 'Helena was back—what use had you for me any more?' she questioned coldly.

'Every damn use!' he exploded.

'Yes, I can imagine,' she retorted and ran up the steps to the front door. She thought she'd never get the key in the lock, her hand was shaking so much. It opened before she could turn it. Helena stood smiling as if she weren't there. She looked past Fran and called to Jordan, 'You forgot your briefcase, Jordan.'

Fran took the opportunity of slipping in the door. She went straight to her room, slammed the door and leaned her back on it, afraid to move, afraid to breathe.

'Fran!' Helena called out later. 'I've made coffee—we need to talk.'

Reluctantly Fran joined her in the high-ceilinged sitting-room. It wasn't a cosy room, it was cold and cheerless on the warmest of days. It was furnished with conventional antiques, nothing out of place, nothing to gladden the eye with surprise. Fran hated the flat, never more than now.

'Fran, I think under the circumstances it would be a good idea if you found somewhere else to live,' her sister said firmly.

Taking the coffee she offered, Fran told her calmly, 'It's already taken care of. I've taken a studio apartment round the corner but I can't pick up the lease till the end of the month. I'm afraid you'll have to put up with me for another few days.' It had been one of the first things she had done when she returned: scoured the papers for alternative accommodation. The rent was

more than she wanted to pay, but a small price
to be out from under Helena's and Jordan's feet.

'I can help with your moving expenses,' she
said, to Fran's surprise.

She looked across at Helena perched on the
edge of a chaise-longue, looked at her properly
and was shocked to see lines of fatigue clustered
round her hazel eyes. For once Helena didn't look
cool and sophisticated at all and strangely, in spite
of her tiredness, she looked younger, even
vulnerable.

Fran looked away from her because something
odd had stirred inside her. She should feel hate
for the sister who was going to marry the man
she loved, but she didn't. She thought she ought
to feel sorry for her too—to love a special sort
of man like Jordan Parry wasn't easy, but you
didn't feel sorry for a woman like Helena. The
feeling confused her and to cover it Fran felt sorry
for herself instead. She was the loser in all this.

'I'm going to bed now,' Fran said, putting her
coffee-cup neatly back on to the tray.

It was as she reached the door that the words
her sister spoke twisted a knife of pain deep inside
her.

'You did the right thing, Fran. You got out
before it was too late. I wish I had had the
strength to do the same.'

No need to ask what she was referring too.

Fran couldn't sleep that night for thinking of
what Helena had said. She didn't look or sound

the contented woman who had won her lover back. She looked sad and regretful as if the fight hadn't been worth it. Helena had seemed convinced that she and Jordan would marry, so why was she so unhappy? Hope swelled inside Fran—maybe Jordan did love her and not Helena.

She flung herself back on the pillows, confused and frustrated. But Jordan hadn't stopped her leaving Paris, or phoned her. She hadn't done those things because he didn't care about her. He *was* in love with Helena. She buried her face in the pillow and cried softly.

It was the day after she moved into her studio apartment that the business news headlines of the paper caught Fran's eye. Jordan's company had successfully bought out Unimet. It was all over.

Fran had picked up the paper on her way to the gallery and during her coffee-break read it avariciously in the back room.

Unimet had at last agreed to Jordan Parry's terms and conditions of take-over. There was a lot about Jordan and Fran read it, her heart in her mouth. The article positively sanctified the man and tears gathered in Fran's eyes. Dr Jordan Parry, a GP who'd given up a vocation to take over the helm of the drug company after his father had been wheelchair-bound after a stroke several years ago. Robert Parry had died and the younger Parry had carried on; ill at ease in the boardroom, he had nevertheless built the company to the exalted trading position it held.

Skipping the share jargon, Fran settled on the part that reported details of the new drug the company had developed, the hormone drug that *she* had so courageously delivered to him in Paris. And whereas Jordan had secured his millions with that drug, she had received nothing but a fractured heart.

It had been developed to help infertility in women. Stress...today's pressures of high achievement...psychological reasons...there were thousands of childless women this drug could help. Fran gulped down her tears as she crumpled the paper in her lap.

How could she have thought him cold and inhuman? Even his negative attitude to Jean-Claude's addiction was understandable. It was an added stress to an already stressful time for him. She shouldn't have burdened him with it. But his treatment of her was unforgivable. He had made her fall in love with him.

Fran sighed deeply. He had forced her into nothing, she only had herself to blame for it all. She had known all along that he could never belong to her. The tinkle of the unobtrusive bell over the gallery door roused her from her thoughts and she went out into the showroom.

'Silas!' she cried in surprise. 'Oh, Silas.' Her heart raced. 'There's nothing wrong, is there? It's not Jordan...an accident...?'

'Good lord, no.' Silas chuckled as he came towards her and took her hands in a reassuring gesture. 'Though your concern is music to my ears.' Fran frowned. 'It shows you care,' he explained. He looked at his watch. 'Is it too early for lunch? I'd like to take you out.'

'Eleven-thirty!' Fran laughed. 'I've just had my coffee-break. Would you like a cup?' she offered. Why was he here? They had formed a good friendship in Paris while she was working for Jordan, but she hadn't expected that relationship to continue now the conference was over.

'If it's not too much trouble. But I would rather like to talk to you in private and uninterrupted.' He looked around. 'Are you alone here?'

'Yes, Ashley the owner is at an auction and won't be back till this afternoon. I'll lock the door and put the closed sign up for a while.'

'You could miss a sale.'

'And I might not.' Fran smiled at him.

She made Silas a coffee in the back office while he sat and flicked through some catalogues. Fran sat across from him and they made small talk until finally Silas let out a sigh.

'I've never had to do anything like this before.'

'Like what?' Fran asked tremulously. She was afraid then. It had to have something to do with Jordan. There was no other reason for his being here.

'Matchmaking. I can't let this continue, Fran. Watch two stubborn people suffer because of their own stupidity.' He leaned forward and took her hand. 'Jordan was devastated when you left Paris.'

Fran stared at him unblinkingly. Of course he had seen the affair between herself and Jordan simmering over those few short days in Paris, but he didn't know about Helena's role in the triangle.

'So devastated he hasn't even contacted me since,' Fran said bitterly.

'You were the one who walked out, Fran. What was the man expected to think?'

Fran shrugged. 'It doesn't matter what he thinks, Silas.' Suddenly her eyes misted with tears and she lowered her lashes. 'I love him and that's why I had to get away. I mean nothing to Jordan. Thank you for trying to patch things up, but it's impossible.' Bravely she forced a smile. 'I can't compete with my sister and it wouldn't be right if I did. I think you should have found out the facts before you came to see me, Silas. Jordan and Helena are going to be married.'

He didn't look at all surprised by her revelation. 'Oh, I did find out the facts before I came here. I know what you believe but you're wrong, you know. There is not going to be any marriage between Jordan and your sister. Poor Helena, so full of her own importance she'd convinced herself she was Jordan's very life support.' He leaned forward and lifted Fran's chin. 'Think about it, Fran. Think of the Jordan you know.

Think about me chasing all over Paris after you because Jordan was sick with worry over you. Think about what he did for your friend——'

'Jean-Claude? What do you mean?' Her eyes widened.

Silas sighed. 'You don't know?' He shook his head sorrowfully. 'Helena should have told you. Maybe it was all too painful for her. She must have realised how hopeless it all was——'

'Silas!' Fran cried. 'You're talking in riddles. I don't understand you.'

He smiled. 'I'm sorry, I'm confusing you, aren't I?' She nodded miserably. 'The morning you left Jordan arranged for that Stella from the art gallery to pay your artist friend a visit, to put a proposition to him. If he agreed, Jordan would arrange and pay for him to attend a drugs rehabilitation centre on the outskirts of Paris.'

Fran clasped a hand over her mouth. 'Oh, Silas...' she breathed, her throat choked with tears.

'It's a private establishment, Fran, the very best help money can buy. Your friend agreed readily enough; he's there now and apparently making good progress. Jordan did that for you, and you think he doesn't care?'

Fran sniffed and wiped a tear from her cheek. 'I didn't know, Silas. Helena didn't say a word to me.' Her voice was low. 'Oh, Silas, that was such a...a good thing for him to do. I gave him such a hard time over Jean-Claude. But...but what did you mean when you said Helena must have realised it was all hopeless?'

Silas leaned back in Ashley's office chair. 'Helena fell for Jordan the first time she joined the company a year ago. She's an excellent secretary, the best the company has had. Jordan was always quick to praise her and I suppose she must have taken it so personally she thought he would eventually fall in love with her.' Silas shook his head. 'Jordan didn't feel that way about her—he lived for his work. Helena was always there for Jordan. She believed that once the pressure was off for him he would see her as a woman and not just a very able secretary. Then Paris happened. Seeing the effect you had on Jordan after you walked out made her realise just how hopeless it was for her. Since Paris she has seen him grow more and more miserable. The strain on her was enormous. Eventually she broke down and told me all about it. How she had felt about Jordan and how sorry she was for the things she had said to you.'

For a while Fran was too choked to speak. She stood up slowly and moved to the coffee-pot and topped up their cups. Part of her was deliriously happy—Jordan did love her—the rest of her felt numb with pain for Helena.

'Help her, Fran,' Silas said softly. 'Her pride is in tatters and she needs you to restore it, to try and forgive her.'

'You really care for my sister, don't you?' she said to Silas as she handed him the sugar. Thank heavens for Silas, Fran thought, at least Helena had him to comfort her.

'I think I must have fallen in love with her the same time as she fell for Jordan,' he told her quietly.

'Oh, Silas, what will you do?' she breathed anxiously.

'I won't give up,' he said with that old sparkle back in his eyes. 'She needs a friend at this moment in time and I'm that friend.'

After Silas had left Fran paced the showroom. She looked at the framed canvases but saw nothing. She wanted to laugh and cry with happiness but life wasn't that simple. Silas had put her mind at rest over Jordan's feelings for her, but he had offered no solution as to how to put it all to rights. Should she phone him, tell him she loved him and ask for his forgiveness? Because it was all her fault. She hadn't trusted him, she'd believed the lies her sister had told. Helena, she needed to talk with Helena first.

That evening she let herself into Helena's flat— she still had her own key. Helena was on the phone in the long hall and she turned in surprise as Fran opened the door.

Fran waited for her in the bleak sitting-room, not sure what she was going to say but knowing things couldn't go on the way they were. They were sisters, and sisters should be friends.

'Fran.'

'Helena.'

They both spoke at once and then a silence yawned between them. Fran moved first, went up to Helena and took her hands. They were cold and trembling slightly. Helena held her head up proudly. She wore the minimum of make-up and her hair was reasonably tidy, but this wasn't the Helena who Fran knew, this was a paler—yes, softer version of her sister. Suddenly Helena's forced proudness crumbled and with a cry Fran took her in her arms.

'Oh, Helena, I didn't realise...I didn't mean... Forgive me.'

The younger sibling comforting the older, Fran's heart was torn with love for her sister.

'Fran, I've been so awful to you. Can you ever forgive me?'

They pulled two wing-chairs up to the electric bar fire and huddled over it, both with their arms clutched tightly around their shoulders. They talked; for the first time in their lives they talked to each other.

'Something inside me snapped when I walked into his bedroom and saw you in his bed. You looked so fresh and innocent, the flush of love still on your face.'

Fran stared at the glowing fire, recalled Jordan's lovemaking, his mouth on hers, his hands intimately caressing her body. The beauty of that had shown on her face. It must have tortured Helena.

'I do understand, Helena. I probably would have reacted the same way if it had happened to me.'

Helena shook her auburn head. 'Not you, Fran, you haven't a cruel streak in you. I was always jealous of you, you know,' she admitted.

'Father told me years ago.' Fran nodded. 'There was nothing I could do about it, I was only a child. When I was old enough I blamed them for your hardness. I could see what they had done to you but they probably didn't realise the harm they were doing. I'm glad we're talking now, we are all the family we've got—each other.'

'We have a lot of years to catch up on, Fran, and it's going to be different from now on.' She sighed. 'I'm supposed to be the mature older sister, but I haven't been very bright where Jordan is concerned, have I?' She shrugged her narrow, elegant shoulders dismissively. 'It's all over now. He's out of my system at last. You gave him that extra something I could never match. You sparked him, brought him alive and then when you left he went out like a candle in the wind. I don't know how he got through the talks in Chicago, he was so low.' She smiled. 'I'm glad Silas came to everyone's rescue. He talked sense into me and made me realise how right you and Jordan are for each other.'

'Silas cares about you,' Fran murmured.

'I know. I care about him too,' Helena sighed. 'Pity I've been blind to it for so long. Maybe somehow I can make it up to him. The time is right for me and Silas now.' She looked over to the grandfather clock across the room. 'You'd better go now, Fran.' She laughed at the surprised expression on Fran's face. 'No, I'm not throwing you out, but you'd better get back to your studio—you're having a visitor soon.' They both stood up and Helena hugged Fran to her. 'I called Jordan just before you arrived, told him the truth, all the awful things I'd said to you. Now he knows the reason you left Paris in such a hurry.'

'You had the courage to do that?' Fran gasped in wonderment.

Helena laughed. 'Crazy, isn't it, that I was more afraid of facing you than my boss? He wants to see you, Fran, so I gave him your new address.'

'He's coming to the studio!' Fran cried, eyes bright with joy.

Helena laughed. 'Don't tell me, you left the place like a tip this morning.'

'Oh, I don't care about that. Oh, Helena, what am I going to say? I just walked out on him ... didn't trust him ...'

'Steady on,' Helena soothed. 'Just be your natural self, it will all work out.'

It wasn't going to work out, Fran panicked when she got back to her own bright studio. She'd honestly expected him to be waiting on the doorstep but he wasn't. She tidied the spacious room with its raised double bed one end and its arched alcove that cleverly concealed the galley-type kitchen the other. She plumped up Aztec-patterned cushions on her Habitat sofa, re-arranged a group of potted plants, sat down, stood up, paced the dhurrie rug on the floor. She almost jumped a foot in the air when the doorbell rang.

He looked wonderful framed in her doorway, tall, dark and achingly handsome in black cords, roll-necked sweater and a soft chunky leather jacket. His smoky grey eyes were tired though, dark-ringed with tension and anguish. He carried a parcel.

Without a word Fran pulled him into the room, linked her arms around his neck and placed her lips on his, and clung to him as if never to let him go. Her love was sealed in the warmth and the depth of that kiss.

'My morning primrose, how I love you,' he husked.

'Jordan, I have so much to say, so many things to tell you——'

He silenced her with his mouth, in a kiss so sweet and perfect she wanted the world to stop at that moment. She drew away at last, breathless and flushed with happiness.

'I love you so much it hurts.' She laughed. 'I'm sorry, Jordan, so terribly sorry for not having faith in you...'

'Don't apologise, Fran. Helena had a lot to answer for...'

'Don't be mad at her, Jordan,' Fran pleaded, her eyes greener than ever with concern. 'She didn't really know what she was saying or doing. She loved you, you see, she was jealous and——'

'And she nearly ruined our lives,' Jordan grated bitterly.

'Did she?' Fran questioned as he slid out of his jacket. She took it from him and hung it up on the bentwood hatstand by the door and turned back to him. He held out his arms and she went to him. 'She couldn't have ruined our lives, Jordan—somehow we would have been drawn back together again. Something as strong and powerful as this doesn't just end because of a lie.'

He laughed then, a soft, loving chuckle. 'What a little romantic you are.'

'Yes, I still dream of orange blossom and white weddings,' she hinted wickedly.

'Then your dream will come true, my darling. But wait.' He went back to the door where he had left the parcel. 'I brought this for you, for us.'

Fran tore the brown paper from the frame and squealed with sheer delight. 'Oh, Jordan! The apple orchard! I love it! I love you!' She flung herself into his arms.

'I bought it the night I first proposed to you,' he murmured in her hair.

She clutched at his shoulders and frowned, but with a laugh in her voice she asked, 'First proposed?'

'I asked you to marry me that first night we met, when we drew up outside the Clermont after dinner together and visiting the gallery. You didn't hear me though, you were too busy screaming abuse at me and whizzing round the revolving doors of the hotel.'

Laughing, Fran shook her head in disbelief. 'I don't believe you!'

'It's true. The next morning I changed my mind, though.'

'You did?'

'I decided I must have had a brainstorm. That was why I wanted you to go home. That evening at the restaurant and Stella's gallery my mind had been assaulted by emotions I had never experienced before. I'd met this crazy young girl, fallen hopelessly in love with her, wanted her so very badly and to top that I was crippled with jealousy when I realised she had an ex-lover in Paris.'

'But I told you there was nothing in it and I didn't want to renew the friendship,' Fran protested.

'Like you, Fran darling, I had no faith.' He pulled her towards him and she laid her fair head on his chest.

'We knew so little about each other,' he went on in a low murmur, 'hadn't had time to build any trust.'

'Oh, Jordan, you're so right. It all happened so quickly.' She lifted her head, her eyes narrowed with concern. 'How do we know everything is going to be all right now? I mean, how long have we known each other? A few days. Is it long enough, long enough to be sure?'

He kissed the tip of her nose. 'I never want to go through these last weeks again in my life, Fran, that I'm positive of. I nearly walked out of the meetings in Chicago, I just wanted to come back to London to find out why you had walked out on me, but the talks would have broken down and they were crucial, Fran, I had to go through with them.'

'Why didn't you call me, Jordan? Just a phone call,' she whispered, aching for the anguish he had been through.

'Fear stopped me. I didn't know then the dreadful things Helena had said to you. I was terrified that it really was over, that you hadn't meant it when you said you loved me.'

'And yet you still went ahead and did that for Jean-Claude. Silas told me you'd arranged for him to have treatment. Although I'd left Paris, you still went to the trouble of helping him.'

'You made me think, Fran, you were so determined to do something for him even though he had stolen from you. I realised that your arguments were right. His actions were a cry for help. It was within my power to do that, so I did.' He kissed her again, slowly and beautifully, but when he drew back from her his eyes had darkened with doubt. 'Fran, you haven't answered my question.'

Dreamily she looked up at him. 'What question?'

'Will you marry me?'

'Oh, darling Jordan, yes, I'll marry you.' She stroked the side of his face to soothe away his worry. 'If I'd have heard I would have accepted the first time, you know. I loved you from the first moment I saw you, struggling with your new glasses and treating me with such shocked rage. You were so stuffy and pompous and so utterly in need of me.'

He gathered her into his arms with such fierce intensity and his mouth on hers was so urgent with need that a rush of desire swept through every nerve in her body.

'And I'm in utter need of you now, my primrose.' He swept her into his arms and headed for the bed. 'We'll plant masses of primroses in the garden of the lodge. You can paint them to your heart's content.' He lowered her down, lay beside her and covered her mouth and throat with kisses. 'They will be a symbol of our love,' he murmured in her ear.

'What lodge?' she uttered weakly, sliding her hands under his sweater, smoothing her fingers over his chest.

'I've bought my little primrose a country home.' He undid the tiny glass buttons of her shirt. 'In Hertfordshire,' he breathed, lowering his mouth to the perfumed hollow at the base of her milky throat.

'Jordan,' Fran moaned, arching herself against him, fires burning deep inside her.

'Yes, my darling?' Sensuously, he removed her blouse from her shoulders, brushing his warm lips across her fiery skin.

'Don't say any more,' she murmured warningly.

He lifted himself up on one elbow and grinned down at her. He smoothed a wisp of golden hair from her temple with sensitive fingers. 'Already I'm picking up bad habits from you, I'm nervous, you see, terrified I'll lose you in the next puff of wind.'

'No fear of that, Dr Jordan Parry. I'll never run away from you again, ever.' She wriggled against him, tantalising him with tiny kisses fluttering around his chin. He responded with a helpless groan.

'Where did you say this lodge was?' she quizzed softly, her excitement growing as his hands caressed her so sensually. 'Hertfordshire...I don't think...no, I've never been to——'

'Shut up, Fran,' he husked as he moved over her. And she did.

POSTCARDS FROM EUROPE
HARLEQUIN PRESENTS

Hi,

Italy, as always, is a model's paradise. But I'm tired of the obligatory parties, the devouring eyes. Particularly those of Nicolo Sabatini, who seems to think I should be for his eyes only.

Love, Caroline

Travel across Europe in 1994 with Harlequin Presents. Collect a new Postcards from Europe title each month!

Don't miss
ROMAN SPRING
by Sandra Marton
Harlequin Presents #1660

Available in June wherever Harlequin Presents books are sold.

HPPPE6

Take 4 bestselling love stories FREE

Plus get a FREE surprise gift!

HARLEQUIN®

PRESENTS Plus

Meet Matt Hunter. He doesn't recognize that Nicola, his new assistant, is the woman who shared his bed one night, eight long years ago. Hardly flattering, but then Nicola has no intention of reminding him of the occasion!

And then there's Grant Goodman. He *must* know about Briony's past, but it hasn't stopped him from hiring her to manage his newest resort in Tasmania. And it may explain his sordid propositions—which Briony could easily ignore if she didn't find Grant so attractive!

Matt and Grant are just two of the sexy men you'll fall in love with each month in Harlequin Presents Plus.

Don't miss

Past Passion by Penny Jordan
Harlequin Presents Plus #1655

and

Unwilling Mistress by Lindsay Armstrong
Harlequin Presents Plus #1656

Harlequin Presents Plus
The best has just gotten better!

Available in June wherever Harlequin books are sold.

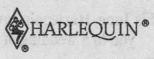

® HARLEQUIN ®

Weddings, Inc.

WEDDING INVITATION
Marisa Carroll

Brent Powell is marrying Jacqui Bertrand, and the whole town of Eternity is in on the plans. This is to be the first wedding orchestrated by the newly formed community co-op, Weddings, Inc., and no detail is being overlooked.

Except perhaps a couple of trivialities. The bride is no longer speaking to the groom, his mother is less than thrilled with her, and her kids want nothing to do with *him.*

WEDDING INVITATION, available in June from Superromance, is the first book in Harlequin's exciting new cross-line series, **WEDDINGS, INC.** Be sure to look for the second book, **EXPECTA-TIONS,** by Shannon Waverly (Harlequin Romance #3319), coming in July.

This June, Harlequin invites
you to a wedding of

Promised Brides

Celebrate the joy and romance of weddings past with
PROMISED BRIDES—a collection of original historical short
stories, written by three best-selling historical authors:

> *The Wedding of the Century*—MARY JO PUTNEY
> *Jesse's Wife*—KRISTIN JAMES
> *The Handfast*—JULIE TETEL

Three unforgettable heroines, three award-winning authors!
PROMISED BRIDES is available in June wherever Harlequin
Books are sold.

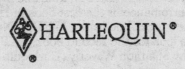

HARLEQUIN®